She Who Trains Under Death

LARRY GENT

ALSO BY LARRY GENT

The Benedict Forecasts
Be All That You Envy (2018)
Never Been To Mars
To Money And A TV
Bedroom Walls That Save Us (2018)

The TOP SECRET Mac Files
She Who Trains Under Death

Avalon Lost
Lightyears To Go Before I Sleep

Vörissa's Catalyst Online
Patch 1.01:   New Game+
Patch 1.02:   Escort Mission
Patch 1.03:   Corpse Run
Patch 1.04:   In Another Castle
Patch 1.05:   Silent Protagonist

She Who Trains Under Death

LARRY GENT

Published in Canada by Midnight Reading Publishing, Ottawa

Gent, Larry, 1983-, Author.
          She Who Trains Under Death / Larry Gent
ISBN: 978-1-989152-01-0
Ebook ISBN: 978-1-989152-02-7
Copyright © 2018 Larry Gent

Cover Design: Valérie Gent

Midnight Reading Publishing
511 Brittany Drive
Ottawa, Ontario
K1K 0S1

Dedicated to Izzy

Because nobody wants to talk about Star Wars, watch Ninja Turtles, have epic snowball fights or participate in water fights with me anymore, but you do!!

That's why you're my favourite!!

CHAPTER 01

The cool autumn air rolled across the city streets. It sent an unsuspecting chill down the bodies of any that it came across. It was the kind of chill that hinted at the end of the summer's patio weather. The patios were mostly empty, the autumnal chill being too much for most, but Bailee didn't mind. The cold rarely bothered her. She'd been in much colder weather for much longer. Bailee MacIntosh sat at the patio table and watched the city pass her by. She sipped a coffee and ate some grilled sandwich, a panini of some sort, and simply enjoyed her meal in silence. It wasn't often that she got to enjoy a meal like this, work rarely allowed a free moment, quiet or otherwise. She had spent so much of her life defending the world that she rarely got to be a part of it.

Bailee MacIntosh was a soldier, one of the best in the world but she belonged to no nation's army. By definition she was a private military contractor, a mercenary, but she always hated that title. Some called her a spy or an operative and some called her a wet worker or an agent. Those titles were no better than the first. Instead Bailee simply called herself Mac.

Mac's eyes fell upon the car parked across the street. It was a red four-door Honda. It had pulled up to a pharmacy and one of the three men inside had gotten out and dashed inside. The other two had stayed where they were. That was ten minutes ago.

Mac wished she could turn it off. She longed for the

ability to shut off her training, to ignore her instincts and simply see the world like others did, but she couldn't. She was like a chef eating at another restaurant. She examined every detail and formed her own conclusion. Except for her the details weren't how a steak was cooked or how the fries were laid out. Her details involved killers, guns and death.

Mac looked at her sandwich and regretted not ordering a steak. It wasn't the food she longed for, it was the utensils. Steaks were served with steak knives. Grilled sandwiches were served with toothpicks. Mac grabbed her fork and slyly slid it up her sleeve. She reached across the table and deviously pulled the glass ketchup bottle closer. She had found the café's use of a glass ketchup bottle charming. Now she found it useful.

The car doors opened and the other two men poured out. Each was dressed in jeans and jackets with their hair buzzed short. They were operatives, the haircuts gave it away. Mac pushed her chair out from the table. She needed room to move when things got hot. Mac glanced to her right. If the two men were in front of her then the third - the one that entered the pharmacy - would be approaching from her right. They were attempting to flank her.

Mac's mind raced as she examined her options. She could fight them here but there were no promises that they wouldn't open fire. Mac had lots of enemies and not all were as concerned with collateral damage as she was. She could retreat indoors and force them into a bottleneck, but a café like this would have cameras and on a busy day like today, someone with a phone was going to record their brawl. Fighting wasn't her best option. Instead, she had to raise the stakes so high that the fight no longer seemed worth it. As they got closer, Mac formulated a plan.

Step 1: Smash the ketchup bottle across the table and toss the remains at the man on her left.
Step 2: Press hands into spilt ketchup before flipping the table to the right.

Step 3: Retreat indoors and start screaming for help like a sick woman. Ketchup stained hands will look like blood.

Step 4: Trip over a table or two and make as big of a scene as possible. Get *everybody's* attention.

Step 5: Escape through rear exit and lure attackers to follow.

Step 6: Fork somebody's eye out.

It was a simple plan but she liked it. Mac liked simple plans.

"Ma'am," the first man said as he got close. Mac slowly slid her hand across the table as she reached for the ketchup bottle. The fight was on. "Are you the one selling the oscillation fan on Craigslist?"

Mac froze. She narrowed her eyes and carefully replied. "That's me. I'm asking $30 for it."

"Would you accept $20? I have it here in cash."

Mac relaxed. It was a code phrase, a way to signal that they were on the same side. These men were from Operations. "Yeah, I'll take $20."

"There has been an incident, ma'am," the lead man said quietly. "We've been ordered to escort you in."

Mac nodded. She stood up and let the fork slide from her sleeve and back onto the table. Her lunch was over. Work had called and it was time for her to save the day once again. She glanced to the man on her right. "You need to work on your approach; you almost lost an eye today."

Mac's escorts drove her to a private airstrip and quickly loaded her onto a Lockheed MC-130J airplane. Twenty-minutes later they were in the air. Mac looked around the plane as it leveled out. The MC-130j Commando II was a Special Forces plane designed to be operated in enemy territory.

This particular plane - the *Trautman* - belonged to the Visegar Company. It was modified to hold more equipment. It could act as an aerial command center for covert operations.

"Thanks for joining us, Mac." She recognized the man who walked towards her. He was Agent Wesley Keane. Mac stood up and shook her hand. "Sorry for the snatch and grab but time was of the essence."

"When isn't it?" Mac said with a smile.

"Tell me about it." Keane said with a smile. Keane was Special Air Service but retired when Visegar's private military gave him a better offer. Mac had worked with Keane in the past and had learned to trust the man. He was tough, strong and smart enough to get out of the field. For the past couple years Keana had been working as a logistical operator. Mac was surprised to see him as a coordinator.

"When did you get the bump to coordinator?" Mac asked.

"I got promoted last month. This is mission number two."

"It's good to see you back on this side of the game." Mac said.

"It's good to be back." Logistical operators were former agents who now worked behind the scenes. They procured and constructed forward operating bases, they helped set up safe houses, laboratories, secure buildings and high security office buildings. Some found the work rewarding but most former agents found it boring. Keane pointed to the younger dark-haired kid behind hm. "This is Agent Grammer Ford. He's working with me. I took him from logistics when I left."

Grammer was a kid in his twenties with an All-American look about him. Mac figured him to be some high school football star in some redneck town. He enlisted in the army and discovered he had a head for soldiering. The brass assigned him to Special Forces and there he stayed until Visegar came a-knocking. Mac had seen his type before. They were always young, strong, and a pain in the ass to deal with.

"I have Polson on the line," Keane said as he escorted Mac to the computer. Keane tapped a button and Operation Manager Rhys Polson appeared on the screen.

"Sir."

"Mac." Polson didn't smile. He was not the smiling type. "Eleven months ago we established a covert research facility on Baranof Island in Alaska. Codename: Morrell Blood. It was supported by a company of our troops. Six hours ago Morrell Blood received a visit from some of our senior staff for a weapons test and inspection. Four hours ago, the base came under attack. Two hours ago, we receive a communications. The attackers have control of Morrell Blood and will execute our senior staff if there is any attempt to retake the base. These attackers are now in possession of numerous top shelf projects. They also potentially have access to sensitive materials. This threat needs to be eliminated and the base needs to be destroyed."

"All company bases are constructed with a remote self-destruct," Mac said. "Why are we not using it?"

"It has been deactivated."

"Aerial attacks?"

"We sent a couple recon drones to investigate but they were shot down." Rhys explained. "They have some sort of unknown anti-aircraft gun."

Mac nodded. Rhys looked at Keane. "I'll leave preparation to you. The mission is a go. I will coordinate from here. Ops is gathering intel as we speak. I will feed you any and all information as we get it."

"Thank you, sir." Keane tapped the keyboard and the window vanished. He looked at Mac and pointed to a locker. Mac nodded and walked over. She pulled open the door and saw a set of combat fatigues hanging inside. Mac peeled off her shirt as she started to change into them. Grammer blushed slightly as he looked away. Mac was a beautiful woman. Her body was firm and well formed. Her skin, however, was decorated with scars. Mac grabbed a sports bra and pulled it on. "What else do I need to know?"

"The attackers are a splinter faction of the Russian Army," Keane said quickly. "They are loyal to General Radek Petrov. They're being led by a Spec-Ops team known as Смертельные Гончие - The Death Hounds."

"What do we know about them?"

"Shit all," Grammer said suddenly. He turned back to face Mac. "We know they are a meta unit but nothing aside from that. HUMINT is gathering what they can."

"Where is my team?"

"DJ and Rath are in Morrell Blood," Grammer said. "They were assigned as protection for the senior representatives."

"What about Cell and Zetes?"

"This is a rapid response mission," Keane said. "Zetes is being grabbed as we speak and as for Cell, nobody ever knows where to find him on down-time. We sent word out through the usual channels."

Mac swore beneath her breath. This was a Spec-Ops led occupation of a covert private military installation that happened to exist in the middle of nowhere. Mac hated how this felt. This was a lone incursion into a highly dangerous situation. This wouldn't be her first mission of the sort but they were far from her favourites. Mac preferred to work as a team; she preferred to work with *her* team. Her Old Man was normally the one they turned to for missions like these. So why hadn't they? Why was she going instead of Gunner Powell? Mac turned to face Keane. She gave him a stern look.

"I need you to be completely open with me, Wesley. I need to know everything."

"I'm learning things just like you are," Keane admitted, "but you have my word. When I know things, so will you."

"So what don't I know that you do?" Mac asked.

"The senior staff's protection detail was handpicked by their accompanying leader," Keane said. "That man was Gunner Powell. I'm sorry, Mac, but one of the hostages is your father."

CHAPTER 02

Mac was a woman who feared little in the world. She had seen the worst that humanity had to offer and yet she still fought for its survival. Yet as she stared at the open hatch in the plane, she couldn't help but develop a hitch in her throat. She breathed deeply through her mask as she waited for the light to turn green. She was about to perform a HALO jump.

"Good luck, Mac," Keane yelled.

"I don't need luck. I have my training." The light flashed green and Mac jumped. She dove downwards as her falling speed grew faster and faster until she reached terminal velocity. Mac tried to steady her breathing as she fell, the wind whipping past her. The wind brought small bursts of pain as it clashed against her body.

The HALO jump (High Altitude Low Opening) consisted of a soldier leaping from a plane flying at a high altitude. The soldier would then free-fall for several minutes, reaching terminal velocity. Only when he reached low altitude would he open his chute and glide to safety. The combination of high downward speed, minimal metal and forward airspeed served to defeat radar as well as simply reducing the amount of time a parachute might be visible to ground observers, enabling a stealthy insertion. The technique dated back to August 16, 1960 when Colonel Joseph Kittinger performed the first high altitude jump. HALO jumps were used to airdrop supplies, equipment and personnel at high altitudes when the threat of a surface-to-air attack was too great.

Mac glanced at the altimeter on her arm and watched the numbers count down. She had leapt at 21 000 feet and wasn't allowed to pull the chute until she reached 2000 feet. She had to free fall until then. Mac looked out over the clouds and found the sun blinding. Above the clouds, with no cover to dull its flare, the sun was unlike anything she had seen before. The sky was a vibrant blue that seemed to illustrate a peaceful world below but Mac knew of the truth. A HALO jump meant battle and no matter how blue the sky was, the world would never be peaceful. Layer after layer of clouds passed her by as she fell. Seconds felt like minutes while minutes felt like hours as she fell. There was little to do during a freefall. All she had to fall and wait.

Her mind raced. How had Gunner gotten caught? The man had both recruited and trained her. Everything Mac knew was because of him. She was good, he was better. Unlike Grammer and Keane, who had been poached from the U.S. Army or the S.A.S., Mac had been recruited from civilian life when she was eleven years old. Gunner found in her an orphanage and took her in. She didn't know it at the time but Gunner had spent days watching her before adopting her. Twelve year old orphans didn't get adopted, it just didn't happen, so when Gunner adopted her Mac was ecstatic. They moved to a country home and the training began. For years he trained her personally, teaching her how to fight, how to move and, more importantly, how to think. He sculpted her into a soldier. He turned from a young and frail Bailee MacIntosh into the Mac she was today. Even at his advanced age, the man could still out-shoot and out-soldier her. How he got caught was beyond her understanding. Unless.... Mac sighed. The only way he got caught was because he wasn't out soldiering; he was out being a bodyguard.

Mac's arm beeped. She glanced at the altimeter and saw her at 2100 feet. She watched the numbers drop. She needed a hundred feet more. As the numbers counted down she reached for the pull cord. When the number hit 2000 she grabbed the ripcord and gave it a yank. The chute opened up and her entire body jerked. Her descent began to slow as she floated towards the trees. Her hope was to steer herself towards somewhere she could safely land but she didn't expect that to be possible. She was setting down in the Tongass National Forest. It was a 17 million acre forest with trees packed densely together. Branches were equally thick and would hurt like hell upon impact. Her landing was not going to be a gentle one.

She winced in pain as she glided into the first tree, branch after branch slamming against her body. She tried to steer away and to turn her body to the side but the branches still hit and they hit hard. A tearing sound filled the air as a branch ripped open her pouch, its contents littering the forest floor below. Mac's body jerked as her chute got caught, halting her descent. Mac twisted in place, trying to free herself but her movement did little but further entangle her. She looked down and saw the ground thirty feet away. Mac shed the shute and lowered herself to the next branch. From there she scampered to the next, and then the one after that until her combat boots hit the dirt. Mac pulled off her respirator mask and let her shoulder length raven-hair fall free. She tossed the mask aside.

Mac slid her bag from her shoulder and examined it. She cursed at the torn pouches. The trees had ripped open the pouch and robbed her of ammunition and grenades. Fuck; of all the luck. She needed every round of ammunition she could carry. She lay out her supplies and did a quick check. She had her MP5 submachine gun and a M17 pistol. She had three mags for the SMG and four clips for the pistol. She had her binoculars, a compass, a GPS, a sat-phone, some food and a black tinted NW Ranger combat knife. She also had her radio. It wasn't a great haul but she'd done more with less.

"*Trautman* this is Raven." Mac spoke through a throat-mic connected to her radio. A throat microphone - or a laryngophone - was a type of contact microphone that absorbed vibrations directly from the wearer's throat by way of sensors worn against the neck. It looked like an expensive set of bluetooth headphones that a jogger wore around his neck instead of his ears. The sensors, called transducers, could pick up speech even in extremely noisy situations or environments. Advance laryngophones could pick up whispers, which benefited her and her need for stealth.

"Go for *Trautman*," Ford replied.

"Raven is on the ground. I lost some of my supplies during the fall."

"What is your location?"

"I landed off target. According to the GPS I am roughly six clicks away from Morrell Blood."

"Proceed with caution, Raven. You are approaching the outskirts of the enemy perimeter. Our drones never made it into that area. They were shot down by some unknown SAM weapon."

"Roger that, *Trautman*," Mac replied. "Raven: out." Mac loaded both of her weapons, holstered her pistol and cradled the SMG. Then she started moving forward. It was a long walk and delaying wasn't going to make it any shorter.

As she moved through the forest, Mac couldn't help but admire the trees. The trees were thick, with greyish-brown bark and leaf-covered branches that shot outwards, each leaf begging for an inch of sunlight to feed upon. Small, brown, makeshift trails decorated the floor. They were worn into the ground from wildlife use.

Gunner had taught her to admire and respect nature. She had guns but nature was still more powerful. Man had conquered the sky but still a plane could be grounded by too much wind or snow. Nature was unstoppable. Humans were simply along for the ride.

Mac was born in Seattle, Washington. She lost her parents when she was only five years-old. They had died in a car accident when their car was sideswiped by a drunk driver in a full-sized pickup. Before Gunner, Mac had spent her entire life in Seattle. When the Old Man took her in, he moved her to Coville, living on the edge of Coville National Park. It was a massive change. For the first week Mac could barely sleep. The wilderness was too quiet. There were no sirens, no street noise and no midnight traffic. How did anybody sleep without all of that? It seemed unnatural. It took a while but Mac eventually adapted, only then did the real training begin.

Bailee's footsteps were slow but they were also careful and meticulous. She'd choose each one with great caution as she moved across the forest floor. She wanted not a single sound to emerge from her movements. She needed to remain stealthy and silent. Bailee knelt down as she inspected the ground. She was tracking the Old Man through Coville National Park. The difficulty of tracking depended on the prey you were following. Some people left hints and signs so blatant that even the most inept tracker could find them but Gunner wasn't one of those people. He would never leave something as obvious as a footstep in the mud or large broken branches. Tracking him required Bailee to be smarter, to look for signs that even he couldn't avoid leaving. As she inspected the ground she saw signs of distress. Grass had been flattened and rocks - albeit small ones - had been disturbed. She was getting close.

Bailee moved forward, her eyes scanning the ground with each step. She scolded herself as she reminded herself to look upwards. The worst thing a tracker could do was to focus on the ground so much that she forgot the world in front of her. Minutes passed as she walked, her gaze moving from the ground to the horizon. Suddenly in the distance she saw him. The Old Man was sitting on a fallen log, happily eat an apple. Gunner had dark hair but very little of it. As long as she'd known the man, his hair line had been receding. He had a circular face, his skin cracked and worn with age, and held himself in a manner he described as a *True Blue Manhattaner.*

Bailee's right hand dropped to her waist holster. She gripped the pistol and effortlessly pulled it free. It wasn't a real pistol, it was a paintball gun made to look and feel like a pistol. Bailee and Gunner were playing a game and the only way for her to win was to track the Old Man, sneak up on him and tag him with a paintball. She had *never* beaten the Old Man before, never, but that was about to change. She leveled the paintball pistol at him and tried to steady her breathing. She was so close to showing the Old Man what she was worth. Her heart raced until the sound of each beat seemed almost deafening. She focused her mind and her body; she would not be beaten, not today.

Crack.

Bailee swore. She was only thirteen and should not have been swearing but she knew that sound and knew what it meant. She glanced down at the broken stick that lay beneath her feet. She snapped her head up towards the fallen log only to find Gunner gone. The Old man had vanished. Bailee swore again. One wrong step and she'd given away her position. She stepped behind a tree and used it for cover as she scanned the wooded area. Where was he? Where had he gone? She swore a third time.

"What have I told you 'bout swearing?" A voice said behind her. Bailee turned around to see Gunner standing behind her, his paintball pistol aimed directly at her. He squeezed the trigger twice and Bailee felt the familiar sting of two paintballs slamming against her chest. "You owe me five laps when we get home."

The loser of the game - and it was always her - was forced to run around the homestead perimeter five times. The property was five acres. Bailee sighed as she lowered her weapon. "Mr. Poole's been wondering why I'm such a good runner."

Mr. Poole was the math teacher at Colville Junior High School. He also acted as the Track and Field coach. He'd had his eyes on Bailee as a long distance runner since she'd transferred to the school for grade seven. She had said no but he continued to pester her.

"So why don't you join? Track would be good for you. You'd be a part of a team."

Bailee rolled her eyes. "Track is lame. I'm already the *outsider girl* without having to be the *outsider girl who runs fast*. Besides, if I start focusing on track then how am I ever going to beat you out here?"

"It takes time, kid. I didn't beat my Dad until I was much older then you," Gunner admitted. "You're growing in skill faster than I ever did. Hell, kid, you almost had me."

"Bullshit," she laughed. "You tagged me a while back didn't you?"

"Watch your mouth," he scolded. A smile broke across Gunner's lips. "Okay, yes. I tagged you a few yards back. It's why I lured you here and littered the place with dry twigs." She understood. If it seemed too good to be true, it probably was. "Also, don't worry so much about your stealth. With practice, you won't need to watch every step. You'll just know how to walk without making a sound."

Bailee rolled her eyes. He kept saying she was getting better but she never saw it. It was like a long dark tunnel. She knew there was light at the end, she could even see hints of it, but it was so far away that she doubted if she'd ever get there.

"Let's go home. You have some running to do and I have some food to cook. How does -" His words were cut short as the familiar sting of two paintballs exploded on his back. "You didn't just...." Gunner spun around and saw Bailee's weapon pointed at him. She'd tried to look stern and serious but a childish laughter quickly broke out on her lips. She'd just shot Gunner in the back, twice.

"Never let down your guard, Old Man."

"You're dead." Gunner snapped up his paintball pistol and snapped off a round but Bailee was already moving. She laughed loudly as she ducked behind a tree.

Paintball was big in Coville, especially with the large matches that happened at the abandoned Air Base, but it was never Bailee's thing. Perhaps it was only a boy thing, perhaps she more interested in other topics or perhaps because she spent dozens of hours each week firing the real thing that she never saw the appeal in the fake. But as she shot round after round of paint-filled projectiles at the Old Man while dodging his round, she couldn't be happier.

CHAPTER 03

"Raven: come in. This is *Trautman* Actual." Keane's voice came over the radio.

"Go for Raven."

"We've got an update on the military force you're coming across," he began. "The forces are the 70th Separate Guard Motor Rifle Brigade. They were a part of the 5th Red Banner Army."

"What the hell are they doing here?" The Russian government, like most nations, wanted to get their hands on meta-humans. They wanted them as part of their military and Special Forces operations but meta-humans were not an easy thing to find. A meta-human was created when the dormant Lycotta gene - a gene found in every human at varying amounts - is activated. Once activated, the Lycotta gene bestowed the individual with super-human abilities ranging from strength, flight, X-ray vision and everything in-between. There were two major entities in meta-research and training. The Visegar Company was one and Polaris Industries was the other. Each was a major corporation with dozens of subsidiaries. If a nation wanted a meta-human, they came to one of the two corporations. The existence of super-human abilities and meta-humans was a major secret that had been kept from most of the world's population. Most governmental agencies planned on keeping it that way.

"Our Russian contacts are denying any involvement.

They are reassuring us of their loyalty to the company," Keane said. "They are also offering any assistance they can."

"Then tell them to come and clean up their own mess."

"They aren't offering *that* kind of help."

"I didn't think so," Mac replied. "What's so special about this General?"

"General Radek Petrov was a trusted senior official of the Russian Ground Forces. He served his entire life. When Russian forces entered Syria during the civil war in 2015, he was the General that led the attack," Keane's voice sounded monotone, like he was reading from a script. "In the couple years following the civil war, Petrov had become more aggressive in his actions. He requested more and more troops, citing the Army of Conquest as a major threat. General Petrov wanted Russia to take further involvement in the conflict. He wanted them to establish fully functional bases. In short, he was looking to invade. "

The Syrian civil war was started in March 2011 and was still ongoing. On one side was President Bashar al-Assad, his government and his allies. On the other side were the Free Syrian Army, the Islamic State of Iraq and the Levant and the Army of Conquest made from several Salafi jihadist groups including the al-Nusra Front. Dozens of other countries got involved in one form or another. The civil war was devastating and caused a global refugee crisis with 6.3 million registered refugees.

"After the Army of Conquest's defeat in early 2017, President Vladamir Putin removed Petrov from the conflict and replaced him with another. Since then, news of Petrov has been scarce. Only recently has word of his quiet removal from the Russian Ground Forces surfaced. He challenged Putin and the President took him out of power. Now he's assembling any forces loyal to him."

"Russia gets into a dick measuring contest and I'm left to clean it up," Mac mumbled.

"That's a very disgusting image, Raven."

"What about the Death Hounds? What do we know about them?"

"We're drawing a bit of a blank on that. The Death Hounds is a name of a previous Spec Ops troop but they disbanded early in the year 2000." The voice on the line was now Grammer Ford. "They were Spetsnaz. The Death Hounds played a big part in the Second Chechen War and were present in the Russian counter-attack in the War of Dagestan."

"Why did they disband?"

"Most of them were killed," Grammer said after a pause. "The Death Hounds were drawing too much attention with their abilities. They were also becoming uncontrollable, the soldiers committed horrible crimes of war like rape and arson. Operations - our Operations - were called in to help quell them. We sent a team to deal with them. One of our agents tracked them to Novya Aldi. There, amidst the horrible massacre, our agent fought and killed nearly the entire team.

"Since that event, the Death Hound unit has been disbanded. Any surviving unit members were disavowed and official record of the unit's existence has been destroyed. Even use of the unit's name is a no-go. The Death Hounds do not exist. If the unit was officially resurrected, we'd know."

"Start cross-checking all known names we have about the previous Death Hounds. I want to know if there is a connection," Mac ordered. "Then send me the last known location of our drones."

Mac kept her MP5 tight to her body as she approached the road. Morrell Blood was located on Baranof Island in Alaska. It was a three hour drive south from the city of Sitka. One of the main economic sources of Sitka was logging. Several logging operations existed on the island. The dirt roads that ran across the island were built so that logging trucks could move in and out of the woods. The Morrell Blood installation was thought by most citizens as just another logging operation. People left the installation alone and nobody questioned why the installation only had two roads from which to enter and exit. There was the north road and the south road. Mac approached the south road and found a massive tree had fallen across it. Mac crept up to the tree and examined it. The log was massive, nearly twice as thick as she was, and once stood thirty feet in the air. She gave it a simply shove and, unsurprisingly, the tree didn't move. Mac moved to the stump. The tree didn't have a rough or violent break. It hadn't been snapped or knocked over by chance. Somebody cut the tree to intentionally cut off one of the two roads. It was going to take several pieces of heavy equipment - or someone like Rath - to move it. The only way a person could escape Morrell Blood was on foot and that would lead them directly into the Tongass forest. Tongass forest was deep, dark and dangerous. Unless they were a trained woodsman, escaping on foot would be more dangerous than being a hostage. Despite her disgust at applauding the bad guys, she found herself impressed. They had effectively cut off any chance of escape. They had locked the base down using little more than a saw.

"Roger that, checking the road now." Mac heard the voice and slinked away. It was the sound of a man's voice speaking into a radio. It was a sentry. Mac backed into the shadows and escaped from view. She quickly readied her weapon and held it by her cheek as she aimed at the tree-covered road.

The sentry stepped into view. He wore a dark green camo combat uniform with a tact-vest and a helmet. He carried an AK-74M assault rifle in his hands. Mac watched carefully. He looked Russian and walked Russian but his voice didn't carry a Russian accent. Mac ignored it. Accents could be faked, hidden or even missed when someone spoke quickly.

Mac wanted to plug the guy full of 9mm rounds from her SMG but decided against it. Her ammo was limited, for one, and killing the first sentry would let every soldier from the street to the base know an attacker was coming. Instead, Mac nervously tapped the trigger guard with her forefinger.

This deep in the woods the MP5 would not have been her first choice of weapon. It had an effective range of only 656 feet and the 9mm round didn't have the power or penetration that the 5.56×45mm did. The MP5 was often used in night operations and close quarter combat. Its small size made it perfect for hostage rescue and escorts. Mac chose it because the plan was that her HALO jump would land her virtually on top of Morrell Blood. The plan called for limited time deep in the woods and more indoor combat. The plan went tits up the moment she leapt from a plane. Now, with limited supplies, the mission had become a POS mission - procure on site. She'd need to find a better rifle or a crap tonne more ammo.

Mac slowly backed away, retreating into the shadows from whence she came. She moved away from the guard until she was satisfied she was safely away. Mac knelt down, pressing her knee in the moist moss that covered the forest floor. She withdrew her phone and glanced at the two files she had received. The first was a list of names. They were the former Death Hounds. She tapped the second file. It was the location of the fallen drone. It was only a half a click away. Mac climbed back to her feet. The drone was shot down. Inspecting the wreckage might give her a hint as to what anti-air the Russians had brought with him.

Mac entered into a small forest grove. She kept her MP5 raised as she crept forward. The grove was eerily silent. There wasn't a single sound that echoed through and that alone made Mac fell uneasy. Nature wasn't quiet; it was bustling hive of action and life. There was always something making noise in nature but the grove was silent. Mac's steps were careful as she looked around. There scratches on the surrounding trees, stillness in the air and, unlike the remainder of the forest, there was no moss on the floor.

Mac spotted the drone's wreckage and walked toward it. She glanced up and saw the damage of the drone's descent in the trees and ground. Mac knelt by the drone and tried to pull it out of the dirt. She ran her hands over the drone's material and she shook her head. The drone was fucked. There was no bullet hole or missile debris. There were simply a scorched exterior and melted metal. Mac withdrew her knife and pried the drone open. Whatever that shot down the drone had fried the device's innards in doing so. If the drone had been shot down by conventional means, there might have been a way to retrieve data but when circuit board and electronics were melted and fried, there was no saving the data. What weapon had the ability to do that?

Dryad lowered her binoculars and smiled. It was a sinister smile that crept across her lips. They had been told to expect someone. There was no way that the company would let an attack like this go unanswered. It was a one-person team and a woman at that. She doubted the boss saw that coming. How much of a threat was this woman and why would they send her alone? She grabbed her radio.

"Base, this is Dryad. Come in base."

"This is Base Actual," a female voice replied.

"We have a target, as expected," Dryad said. "How should we proceed?"

"Observe for now." The voice was firm and commanding. "I'll send backup."

"I can handle this on my own," Dryad protested.

"Do as you are told," the voices snapped, "and hold position. Reinforcements are on their way. Base out."

Dryad scowled. She wanted to go down there and rip the woman's arm off. She wanted to prove that she was more than simply a utility member of the team. Dryad raised her hand. A small breeze appeared out of nowhere and brushed past her fingers. She would prove herself.

A breeze appeared from nowhere and blew past Mac. The hairs on her body stood on end. She narrowed her gaze as she raised the MP5. She glanced at the grove and cursed herself for missing it. The scratched trees, the flattened earth and the moss-less forest floor; there was a reason for each and that reason had just entered. Mac felt it on the wind before she even heard it. It was big, it was dangerous and it had just come to see who was in its grove.

Mac turned around slowly, not wanting to make any sudden moves. She looked across the grove and found herself locking eyes with a grizzly bear. A female grizzly stood over nine feet on its hind legs and weighed upwards of 400 lbs. Most grizzly bears had brown fur with blond tipped fur. This bear had blond hair with brown tips. Mac cursed to herself. All she had on her was the MP5 and the M17. Neither of which was going to kill a bear like this. It was only going to piss it off.

Mac backed away slowly, fearing the result of any sudden movements. The bear growled and stomped, shaking its fur for all to see. The bear was acting very aggressive. Bears weren't aggressive for simply no reason. Something was wrong and Mac didn't want to find out what had been stupid enough to piss off a grizzly. Mac moved quicker as she exited the grove. There was no right way to fight a bear. There was no right way to run away from a bear. The only right thing to do was to avoid the bear all together.

Mac glanced at her phone as she examined the map.

She knew she was at the barrier of the Russian's patrol, the guard at the road told her that, but she had to plan the next approach carefully. She pinched her screen and made the map expand. The topographic map of the area showed Cliffmont Edge. It was a small cliff. If she made her way there, she might be able to get a better view of lay ahead of her. Without an aerial view or an overhead scan by a drone, she had no intelligence available to her. She was winging it and so far it was working but she couldn't last like this. The key to success was preparation.

Cliffmont Edge was a slanted hill that grew upwards. At its peak it stood fifteen foot in the air. Mac climbed upwards. With each step the air seemed to grow colder. It nipped at her skin and assaulted her senses. The higher she got, the more the air felt foreign. Mac clutched her weapon tighter. She had learned a long time ago that when something didn't feel right, there was often a real reason behind it. As Mac reached the peak, the air suddenly became freezing cold. It felt like the winter bite.

"You are not him," a Russian voice said. Mac turned around, her weapon at the ready. She glared at the Russian man.

"You're smart and observant," Mac said sternly. "I've never been a *him*."

"We expect someone to come but we did not expect one like you," the Russian said. "Who are you?"

"Does it matter?" Mac asked. Condensation escaped her lips. She was cold and she had her suspicions as to why. She lined her sites onto the Russian man's skull and put her finger over the trigger. Mac shifted her stance and put a light bend in her knees.

"I guess not." The man stepped forward. "I am the point man for the Death Hounds. My name is Morozko."

"Stupid name." Mac eyed the man. He was tall, standing at nearly 6'7. He had large hands, piercing blue eyes and had a bald head beneath his black barrette. She saw the green sling that hung around his chest and slid towards the rear.

"Perhaps but it was one assigned to me for obvious reasons. Now, you and I need to have a talk about --" Mac opened fire. A burst of three 9mm rounds shot forward but Morozko didn't flinch. His left hand shot upwards as a shield of ice formed around his palm. The bullets dove into the ice, becoming stuck and leaving the Russian free of harm. Morozko just smirked. Mac kept her face firm. An ice-meta, she had suspected as much. Mac stepped forward, firing another burst. Morozko brought forth another shield of ice and grunted in surprise. He hadn't expected the woman to fire so quickly and without hesitation.

Morozko raised his hand and quickly formed a wall of ice several feet high. It would slow the woman down or so he thought. Seconds later Mac reappeared, leaping over the wall. Her foot slammed into the Russian's chest and both went toppling down the edge. Mac was on her feet first, swiftly rolling to her knees before leaping upwards, but Marozko quickly followed. Mac struck with the butt of her SMG but the Russian pivoted away. He grabbed the MP5's barrel with his left hand and willed it to freeze. The black barrel turned blue and snapped in Mac's hands.

Fuck. She needed that.

Mac let go of the weapon and lunged for Morozko. She grabbed his left arm and twisted. Her right knee shot upward and twice slammed into his gut. Morozko doubled over but Mac didn't let up. She shifted her feet, knocked the man off balance and rolled him over her hip, tossing the man directly into the ground.

Morozko scrambled to her feet. He flashed a wicked grin. "You are very good, *Zaika*, very good indeed but being *very good* won't be enough for today."

His fists were blurs as a series of jabs flew towards her head. Mac's hands moved swiftly as she slapped aside the blows. Morozko's height made the punches difficult to deal with. Mac was 5'10. There was an eight inch difference between the two which made each punch a descending cannonball aimed directly at her head. Mac slapped aside the two light jabs before ducking under the swinging right. Mac struck Morozko's side twice and kicked out his leg. She spun and slammed her left fist across Morozko's face. Mac's eyes went wide as her fist ached in pain. It was like she had punched steel or --- ice. She had just punched ice.

Morozko spun and grabbed Mac. He locked her arm in a Sambo hold and held her in place as he slammed fist after first into her side. His fists were covered in ice and it hit much harder. Mac had faced off against the biggest of the bads and she was still standing. She had faced men who had ten times her strength and women who could fire a dozen punches in the blink of an eye. She had faced each and bested one after another and sent each packing. Yet here she was, off guard and out classed. She walked into an ambush. She had been tossed into the deep end of the pool and was frantically kicking to stay afloat. She needed an out and she needed it now. Mac shifted her arm and heard a familiar cracking sound. She winced in pain as her shoulder popped out of its socket. Mac twisted her body, drew her black knife from her holster and stabbed it deep into Morozko's leg. The Russian screamed in pain. He spun his body around and pitched Mac through the air and up Cliffmont Edge. She smashed through has glacial wall and sent shard of ice flying everywhere. Mac hit the ground and rolled to her feet. Her first reaction was to draw the pistol at her side and put a bullet between the Russian's eyes but as she saw the Russian reached for the gun hanging from the sling around his neck, she quickly changed her mind. Morozko drew a PP-2000 and leveled it at her. The PP-2000 was a Russian made SMG. It was used mostly by the Russian Ministry of Internal Affairs and Armenian Special Forces. The PP-2000 only had an effective range of 328 ft but it also had the ability to fire thirteen rounds every second. At this close range she was outgunned. Morozko leveled the weapon and squeezed the trigger. In less than a second, thirteen 9mm rounds were flying towards her. Mac had nowhere to hide and nowhere to dodge. She only had one option. Mac turned around, dove for the ground and rolled off the side of

Cliffmont Edge. She fell the fifteen feet and slammed down on the ground below. Morozko blinked. He hadn't expected that. He ran to the cliff's edge and stare over it. He expected to see Mac lying on the ground but instead there was nothing but the dirt and forest floor.

Mac was nowhere to be seen.

"Run, little *Zaika*," Morozko taunted, "run as far as you can and you may just survive the day."

CHAPTER 04

Bailee looked out of the passenger window and froze. She saw a truck barrelling towards her. In that moment before the crash, time seemed to slow for the fourteen year old girl. Gunner was driving Bailee in his Land Rover. Bailee kept calling the vehicle a Jeep but Gunner was quick to correct her. It was a Land Rover and there was a major difference. Bailee couldn't see any but she had learned a while ago not to argue with Gunner on trivial matters. She saved her strength for the big fights.

Gunner was driving to a mountain cabin. He had picked her up from Junior High. It was the middle of winter and the jeep had hit a patch of black ice. The Land Rover spun out but Gunner quickly regained control. He pulled the Rover to a halt so he could check that Bailee was okay. That was when the truck slammed into them. The driver wasn't drunk; he just lost control on the icy roads.

In the moment of slowed perception, Bailee was assaulted with every flashback and their accompanying fear. She had lost her parents to a car accent. Was she going to lose Gunner to the same method? Or had fate decided to claim her in the same fashion as they had claimed her parents? The pickup's driver tried to slam on the breaks but the ice had robbed him of control. Bailee could do nothing but watch as the pickup slammed into the side of the Rover, all in slow motion. The pickup pitched the Rover onto his side, off the guardrail and gravity did the rest. The Rover rolled down the hill until it came to a crashing halt.

"Bailee! Bailee! God, fucking no, please. Bailee!" Gunner voice was the first thing Bailee heard when she came to. His voice was loud and rough, like he had been screaming for several moments. Bailee groaned as she tried to assess her situation. She was pinned in the upside down Rover. The seatbelt held her in her chair. Her left arm was numb and her head hurt but she was still alive. Her passenger door suddenly snapped opened. Bailee looked up and saw Gunner standing there with a crowbar in his hand. The old man dropped the bar and drew a knife. He always had a knife. He quickly cut away the seatbelt and freed Bailee from her bonds. He pulled her out of the car and into the snow. He leaned in, tears in his eyes, and kissed her on the forehead. "Oh thank God, Bailee. You're okay."

"Gunner?" she murmured. The old man just nodded as he pulled her close. She cried out in pain as the hug put pressure on her left arm. She pushed away and took a good look at her adoptive guardian. He was bleeding from several points on his head and face and his clothes were torn. Yet aside from all of that, Bailee couldn't help but focus on the tears rolling down his cheek. It was a rare sight. "I thought men didn't cry."

"Shut the fuck up, kid" he said. "I'm just happy you're okay."

"My arm," Bailee whimpered. "It hurts, it hurts bad."

"Let me take a look." Gunner gently ran his hand over Bailee's arm. The left shoulder hung lower than the right. Gunner ran his down to her left hand, only to find it a bluish colour. "Can you move it?' Baile tried but found herself only gasping in pain. She looked up, fear in her eyes, and shook her head.

"What's wrong with me?"

"Your shoulder is dislocated. It's a minor threat, at best, in the injury world," Gunner said. His face dropped. "The bad news is we have to deal with it here."

"Why can't we wait until we get to a hospital?"

Gunner pointed up the ice covered cliff side. Bailee could see the damage that the Rover had caused. The fall was a long one and the climb back up was going to be difficult, even in the best of health. With only one arm it was going to be impossible.

"This is going to hurt. I'll do it on three," Gunner said as he grabbed her arm. "One..."

Gunner jolted and Bailee screamed.

Mac huddled in the forest, safely away from Morozko. She leaned up against a tree and examined her body. Her left arm was numb. Mac ran her hands over it and sighed. She had dislocated her shoulder, again. Mac had been on the receiving end of broken bones, concussions and chasm-deep lacerations but the one injury that annoyed her most was the dislocated shoulder. It was the inconvenient hurdle that sprung up and put her out of commission for a couple days. In a perfect world she would spend a couple days recovering from a dislocated shoulder. She didn't have a couple days. She didn't even have time to get a medic to look at her. She had to deal with her wound on her own.

Mac kept her left arm tight against her body with a 90° bend at the elbow. She rotated the arm away from her body until she felt a resistance. Then she pressed her shoulder against the tree. This was called the Kocher's Method. It was thought to be three thousand years old. This timeline was estimated from wall painting in the Egyptian tomb of Ipuy that appeared remarkably similar. When done with a second person the technique proved to be painless. When done alone, it hurt like a bitch.

Mac took a couple deep breaths. She was going to press against the tree while rotating her arm outward. The leverage would pop the shoulder in but it was going to hurt. She resolved to do it on three. Mac began to count. One --

Mac slammed her shoulder against the tree and screamed as her shoulder popped back into place. She dropped to her knees. She never made it three. It was tradition after all.

"*Trautman* this is Raven, come in."

"This is *Trautman*," Grammer's voice replied. "You okay?"

"Yeah, I'm fine now." She dropped to the ground with a plop. She pulled off her bag before leaning on the tree. "Get Actual, I have an update."

"He's here, go ahead."

"I just faced off against a meta. I was forced to retreat." Mac pulled open her bag and withdrew a chocolate bar. It was a Snickers. She smiled. She always got a little beat up when she was hungry. She tore open the wrapper and took a bite. "His name is Morozko. He's an ice-meta."

"We're searching now, Raven."

"He's 6'5, bald and Russian," Mac continued between bites. "He said he was their point man. See if that helps."

"Morozko is a name of a Russian Fairy Tale," Grammer said over the radio. "He's an old ice man who lives deep in the forest. If you treat him politely and with kindness he rewards you with a chest full of fine thing and nice garments. If you are rude to him then he freezes you to death."

"Guess I was rude," Mac admitted with a smile. "Anything else?"

"Aside from the message that step-mothers suck," Grammer said. "The fairy tale doesn't tell us much more. We'll search our database and see if we can find a match. Any other details?"

Mac silently chewed on her Snickers bar as her mind raced. She had a theory but not one she was ready to admit. "How are things on your end, Actual?"

"It's not mission critical, Raven," Grammer said. Mac rolled her eyes. Grammer was one of *those* coordinators. He was a *need to know* man and in his opinion she didn't need know. A few moments later he returned.

"Russians are pissed at us," he reluctantly admitted. Mac smiled. Keane had just scolded him for keeping intel from her. "They are pissed that the Company would automatically accuse them of running this attack. To be honest, I don't know how our business relationship will be after this."

"That sounds like Retention's problem," Mac laughed.

"Basically, Raven."

"I've lost my primary weapon," Mac admitted as she took the last bite. She grabbed her canteen and opened it. She took a long swig of water. "I'll have to acquire another one here."

"Are you unarmed?"

"Negative. I still have my M17, *Trautman*." Mac drew the pistol. The M17 was a modified SIG Sauer P320. It was compact pistol that could be modified using different modules and accessories. The compact pistol was built with a polymer grip frame modules that allowed the possibility to interchange the chamberings. Mac's M17 had a tactical light on the bottom and a silencer attached to the barrel. She gave her weapon a once over and made sure it was ready for a fire fight. "I will acquire a rifle on site."

"Just be careful, Raven. We still need you."

"You always do, *Trautman*," Mac said with a sigh. She packed her bag and slung it over her shoulder as she stood up. "You always do. I'll keep moving. Send me updates when you get them. Raven out."

Mac drew her knife as she climbed to her feet. She held the M17 in her right hand and the blade in the other. She held them close, one supporting the other. Mac had to be careful. She had lost the element of surprise. The Death Hounds knew she was there. They, along with the 70th Separate Guard Motor Rifle Brigade, would be on the lookout for her. The worst part was any doubt she had of multiple meta on site was now confirmed by Morozko's appearance. Metas were like a rook or a queen. You simply did not send them out to die and you certainly didn't send them that far away from the objective. The fact that they sent the ice-man so far away from the hostages meant that Morozko wasn't the only meta. The fact that they were willing to send him out meant that he wasn't even their strongest meta, a fact Mac hated even more.

In the middle of Gunner's living room was a big comfy chair. It was a distressed red - a colour that didn't match with else in the place - and had thick cushions that swallowed a person whole. It was Bailee's favourite chair. When she sat in it, she felt how she assumed a caterpillar did when nuzzled in a cocoon. Bailee sat in the chair and she read. She held in her hand a worn paperback copy of a book Gunner had assigned her. At first she just watched the movie and passed that off as reading. Gunner knew right away and scolded her for it. The movie, as she was quickly discovering, was *nothing* like the book save for a few names. So, she sat in her favourite chair and read *Starship Troopers*. She hated every moment of it.

The book was such a *guy book*. It was all about war and soldier and hoo-rah this and boo-yeah that. To make matters worse, the book was very fascist. Everything the people did had to be for the betterment of the nation. Everything was for the betterment of the military. Only the best could vote and to be the best you had to serve the nation. Stupid *guys books*.

"How the book, Kiddo?" Bailee looked up as Gunner entered the room eating an apple. She sighed at his question.

"If you're raising me to be a fascist, you better tell me now. I have a lot of communistic beliefs that I'll have to purge, Comrade," Baille joked. "Also I'll have to remove my hammer and sickle patches off of every one of my red shirts. I mean, unless there is a person we know that will do that for me if I tell them it's for the betterment of the nation."

"Smart ass," Gunner said, smacking Bailee's foot with his hand. He pulled up a stool and plopped down upon it. "Is fascism the only message you got from this book?"

"Um...war is good?" Bailee suggested. Gunner frowned at her. Bailee hated that frown. It was a look of disappointment, a look that said *I know you can do better*. "I think the author is saying war isn't something fun, like in games or those movies. War is something that sucks and has to be endured. I also think he's saying that we have to do whatever we can to keep it away from our home. It's a kind of *we fight them there so we don't have to fight them here* type of scenario."

"What was the last book I made you read?"

"*Animal Farm*."

"All animals are equal but some are more equal than others," Gunner recited. "And the book before that?"

"Was it *Nineteen Eighty-Four* or *Brave New World*?" she asked. "Your book choices are boring, Old Man."

"But they are necessary," he said. "I'm training you for a great deal. I teach you how to fight, how to shoot and how to survive but all that will do you no good if I don't teach you how to think."

"Yeah, you don't want me making any thought crimes in this house," she sarcastically added. Gunner shook his head.

"It's not like that. I'm not trying to tell you *what* to think. I'm trying to show you *how* to think. You need to learn for yourself how to look at the world around you and make your own decisions.

"You are about to be brought into a complicated and scary world. It's a world where you are the weakest link. It's an unfair world where everybody will be naturally better, faster and stronger than you. You will have the odds majorly stacked against you. I just want to give you a fighting chance."

Bailee receded into her chair. "If you're trying to scare me, it's working."

"I'm just being truthful. This world of ours holds a very dark secret. It's one that only a fraction of the world knows about and we intend to keep it that way." Gunn paused as he prepared his next words. "Bailee, this world has super powers." Bailee eyed him suspiciously.

"There is a gene in all of us called the Lycotta Gene. Different people have different amounts. The Lycotta Gene has one purpose: to keep us alive. It does it by unlocking hidden abilities within us. When you are fighting for your life and all seems lost, there is a chance the gene will activate. For some it will give temporary strength, stamina or speed but for others it changes them permanently. This gene has made men super strong, it was made women super fast and it has even given one guy I know the ability to shoot eye beams."

"You're bullshitting me."

"No, Kiddo," Gunner said with a shake of his head. "I'm not. You know my friend Jason from work? He can move objects with his mind."

"Does this mean I'll get powers?" Gunner shook his head.

"I had you tested. Your Lycotta count is too low. The odds are you will always be just a regular human. That's why we train, so if the need arises *we* can take *them* down. Powers aren't a blessing. They are a curse. Nine times out of ten, powers will mess the person up. It's a dark and horrifying thing when a meta goes bad. So we fight them there, in the dark corners of the world, so they don't fight here, in the light where everybody can see them."

Bailee wrapped her arms around her legs. Tears formed in her eyes as anger made her chin quiver. "Is that why you adopted me? So you could train me to fight in your stupid fucking war?" The words exploded out of her mouth. Her voice was filled with rage and sorrow. "You didn't care for me at all; you just want another fucking soldier."

"That's not true," Gunner said calmly. He became fidgety in his seat and began to run his hand through his dark hair, what little he had. "I was lonely. I needed someone to share my life with. Having a kid wasn't possible for me so I adopted."

"So why train me?"

"I raised you the way I did for two reasons. The first one being that my world deals with metas. Like it or not, you are going to get pulled in. I want to make sure you can stay safe when you do."

"And the second?"

"It was the only way I knew how to raise a kid," Gunner sheepishly admitted as he tossed his core into a trashcan. "This was how my dad raised me."

"What happens if I don't want to be a part of your war?"

"Then I help you be a part of whatever world you want. You want to go to school? I'll make sure you get in. You want to enlist? I will help you get the best recommendations. You want to start your own business? I will be your very first customer." Gunner leaned forward and took Bailee's hand into his own. "Whatever you want to do in life, it's my job to help get you there. I just have two rules: no drummers and no sushi."

Bailee cracked a small smile. "So you actually love me?"

"I loved you from the moment I saw you, Kiddo."

Bailee dove into Gunner's arms and the two held each other. They weren't the hugging type but at that moment - that very awkward moment - it felt right.

"So what's the weirdest power you've seen?" Bailee asked as she withdrew herself from his arms.

"I know a guy who shoots pies from his wrist."

"Really?" Bailee caught herself a moment later. "You dick."

"Seriously though," Gunner said between laughs. "I know a guy who can replicate himself. He walks around with like twenty copies of himself and runs a taxicab company. Each car is driven by an exact copy of himself."

"Freaky."

"It gets better," Gunner laughed. "They each date different women."

CHAPTER 05

Mac's boots slowed to a halt as the sounds of rustling leaves reach her ears. She raised her pistol to eye level as she lowered her body down to one knee. She spotted a trio of soldiers approaching. She was safely hidden from their view but she kept her weapon trained on them as she reviewed her options. Her M17 held a silencer. With her speed she could drop all of them before they notice anything was wrong. Mac lowered her weapon. There was no point killing them when she could sneak around them. Mac had killed before, every soldier had, but she tried to avoid it at all cost. Soldiers rarely went to places of their own accord.

Mac leapt from shadow to shadow as she snuck around the guards. She moved past the patrol and crept into a small building. From the outside it looked like a small lunchroom for loggers, a hut for them to stop mid day and have a snack in, but as Mac pushed open the door and crept inside, she realized the outside was simply a facade. The inside was a guard station. It had multiple weapon racks, a radio and several boxes of ammo. Mac raised an eyebrow. This was definitely a Visegar base. This was a medical site but Visegar also made sure that nobody could access their covert research. They protected their high assets and covert location with Visegar's own private military. Operations was a division of Visegar's private military.

Mac moved through the building. She checked rack

after rack, frowning as she found each empty. Her eyes lit up as she noticed several empty pistol magazine, numerous rifle mags and two boxes full of 9mm rounds. She grabbed the mags and found her good luck fade slightly. They were mags for a Browning. There were not compatible with her M17. Mac shrugged and returned them. At least she had the ammo. She slid the boxes into her bag and kept searching. Mac paused at the radios and glanced at the device. It was an elaborate radio that had a built in scrambler. The scrambler made it so any incoming transmissions were gargled and un-decipherable unless the proper five-number code was put in. Mac eyed a piece of paper beside the radio. It held a list of five-digit numbers.

- 12085
- 12048
- 14015
- 14112
- 14180
- 14025
- 14252

The numbers were most likely various encryption codes but Mac didn't know if they belonged to the Russians or Visegar. Mac turned to leave when the glimmer of black gun-steel caught her eye. She crossed the room until she found it. Mac smiled. There, abandoned on the floor, was a M4 carbine rifle. Mac picked it up and ran her fingers across the frame. A M4 was the weapon of her choosing. Unfortunately, this M4 didn't have all the bells and whistles. It was a basic rifle with a holographic sight attached but in her hands it was more than enough. She had found her new rifle.

"Hey," a voice said suddenly. Mac heard the sound of a rifle being pointed at her. She turned around to see one of the three soldiers standing in the doorway. He aimed an AK-74M at her. "Don't move."

Mac did as she was told and didn't budge. The soldier

moved a few paces inward, circling around to her left. It was a smart approach. Only 12% of people were left-handed and even less when it came to women. It was a fair assumption that he was approaching her on her weak side. The twist was that he wasn't. Mac didn't have a weak side. She was perfectly ambidextrous.

"Drop the gun." Mac did as she was ordered. She dropped the M17 on top of the table beside her. "Now get on your knees." Mac didn't budge. "Get on the ground!"

Mac glanced at the soldier and flashed him a defiant smirk. It was the type of grimace that challenged the man and simply said *make me*. A flash of anger passed through his man-brain and he marched closer. He had just been challenged and by a woman. There was no way his macho man-brain was going to allow that. It was a predictable response in male soldiers and one that he would regret the moment he stepped within arm's reach.

"I said get on the---" Mac's left hand shot out and grabbed the AK's barrel. She twisted it counter-clockwise and pushed it away from her. Mac's right foot shot out and kicked on his left knee. The soldier was startled and accidently squeezed the trigger. A pair of rounds shot off. Mac swore. In the distance she could hear the sound of yelling. The remaining two soldiers were going to be coming through that door in less than sixty seconds. It was her job to make them regret that choice.

Mac slammed her right hand into the soldier's side and then again into his neck. He made a choking/gagging sound as she assaulted his Adam's apple. Mac grabbed him by the back of his head and pulled her knee upward into his gut. Mac pulled down on his head as he doubled over, slamming his head twice into the top of the table. Mac kicked out his leg and watched as the soldier's body crumpled. She snatched her M17 off the table and leveled it at the door. She squeezed the trigger twice as soldier #2 entered the room. She put a 9mm round in each leg and watched as he fell. She fired another pair and put two rounds into the shoulder of soldier #3. Mac lowered her weapons and put a round into the left leg of soldier #1, just to be safe. She turned to the radio and put one more round into it. She didn't want backup.

Mac slipped the M4 ammo into her bag before grabbing the rifle. She moved to door and paused. He glanced down at soldier #2. He was the only one still awake. The other two were either knocked out or had blacked out due to the pain. She grabbed the first-aid kit and held it before his eyes.

"How about a trade?" She dropped the kit on his chest and in exchange she took a pair of grenades from his belt. She pocketed the frags. "Pleasure doing business with you."

The forest became still once more as Mac walked and all sound seemed to peter off into silence. The sound of Mac's beating heart almost seemed deafening in her ears. Mac tightened the grip on her weapon as she looked around for the cause. From her left she heard the sound of a low growl. Mac pivoted and raised her M4. She locked her sights onto the form of a snarling wolf.

The wolf was two feet tall and three and a half feet long. They had dark grey fur with a brownish pattern that travelled down its back. This was no ordinary wolf. This was an Alexander Archipelago wolf. Mac lowered her weapon. She wasn't going to shoot a wolf - especially not an endangered one - and if she were, the wolf in front of her wasn't the biggest threat. Mac quickly glanced to her left and right. She couldn't see them but she knew they were there. No wolf hunted alone, especially a wolf so close to a Grizzly's grove.

"Easy boy," she whispered. "I'm not here to hurt you and I know you're not here to hurt me. So why don't we just go our separate ways and leave each other be." The wolf didn't budge. It simply growled. "Why are you here?"

Unsurprisingly, the wolf did not answer.

Mac knew more about wolves then she'd ever thought

necessary. Gunner admired the wolf. He was obsessed with them. If the Old Man believed in spirit animals, the wolf was his. If Mac believed in spirit animals, hers would be whatever animal would make fun of Gunner for believing in spirit animals.

The wolf lowered its body, like it was about to pounce, and let out a deep growl. Mac lowered her stance, like she was ready to fight, and she let out a growl of her own. She was the alpha, not this wolf and Mac was ready to prove it.

The wolf growled.

She growled back.

Both locked eyes and neither moved. Mac never raised her rifle; she kept it pointed at the ground. For several moments, the standoff continued. Mac knew it was a bad idea to keep focused on the wolf in front of her while two more had her flanked but she had no other option. She doubted she could fight her way out. She estimated that she could kill two wolves before the third ripped her throat out. She couldn't throw herself at the mercy of the animal like she did with the bear. Wolves and bears were very different creatures. Instead, she had to prove herself worthy to these wolves. She had to prove herself the alpha.

Dryad watched as the wolves retreated. She stared in shock. How was that possible? The wolves had her flanked. They had her dead to rights. She expected a fight, a desperate attempt before she died by tooth and claw but there wasn't one. The woman hadn't even bothered to raise her damn gun. She just stared them down, growled and the wolves turned tail.

Who was this woman?

"Dryad to Base."

"Go for Base."

"Target found. Relaying location."

"Good work. Don't lose her this time. Base out." Dryad snarled. She didn't lose the target, Morozko did. She was the one cleaning up the bastard's mess, again. She often wondered, after all of his messes, if the benefit of the ice-Russian outweighed his cost.

Mac reached the edge of Morrell Blood. She crouched down by a tree and lowered he weapon. She withdrew her phone and brought up her map of the base. Morrell Blood was built to look like a logging base. The reality was highly different. Morrell Blood was essentially broken into quarters. Mac glanced down at her map. The north-west corner was the armoury and weapons. The south-west quadrant was the vehicle bay. Barracks, sleeping quarters and offices were in the south-east. The north-east corner was where the scary shit happened. The north-east corner held Visegar's science labs. Mac didn't know where the hostages were. Whatever AA weapon they had, it robbed Ops of the chance to get intelligence. Mac pocketed her phone and withdrew her binoculars. She scanned the base from afar. If they were holding hostages in one of the buildings, there would be signs. The dorms had guards at every entrance, several on the roof and she could see multiple forms walking past the building's windows. If she was a gambling woman - and Mac was, except on missions - she would put a healthy amount of chips on the dorms.

A flash of light caught Mac's eye. She spun her binoculars downwards and saw a small group of Russian soldier standing in a gaggle. In the middle was a black-haired man. He walked in circles, talking loudly and vibrantly. He held his two hands palm upwards, like they were scales. A ball of lightning leapt from one hand to another. Mac frowned. Lightning metas were always a pain her ass. Mac grabbed her phone and swiped upwards for the camera. She zoomed in as much as her phone would allow and focused on the meta. She snapped a few pictures and sent them to Keane.

"Raven this is *Trautman* Actual."

"Go for Raven."

"We got your pictures. What are we looking at?"

"It's a lightning meta." Mac starred once more through her binoculars. The meta wasn't dressed in army combats. He was dressed in clothes that made him look more like a private military contractor then Spetsnaz. "I know the picture isn't great but hopefully tech can clean it up."

"We'll look for a facial match and see what we can pull up," Keane said. "What your next plan?"

"I'm thinking the hostages are in the dorms. I'm going to sweep around towards the vehicle bay and see if I can get a better look inside the dorms." Mac lowered the binoculars. Something was wrong with the soldiers. The one guarding the perimeter looked Russian but the further in to Morrell Blood she peered, the less uniform they looked. Instead of combats they wore jeans and jackets. "I have a hunch I need to investigate."

"Roger." The radio went silent for a moment. Seconds later Grammer's voice replaced Keane's. "Have you spotted the AA weapon yet?"

"I think I just sent you a picture of it," Mac joked. "Where did Actual go?"

"He had another call," Grammer answered. "You think the zapper is acting as an AA?"

"The circuits were fried and there was no projectile weapons damage. I think he zapped it out of the sky."

"Zappers are fairly common in the powers lottery so a meta search will be difficult. If you have any more details keep us informed."

"Will do, *Trautman*." Mac was quiet for a moment as she tried to word her next question. "Who chose security detail?"

"The file showed that Protection Services - PS - assigned the detail."

"PS doesn't normally pull from Ops and they *never*

pull from Black Bag," Mac said. "Who the hell are these hostages?"

"That's classified," Ford said.

"Just tell me or put Actual back on the line," Mac sighed. Grammer reluctantly replied.

"The names are coded out but if my sources are true, then Agent: Blindspot is Tier 4 management."

Mac swore. Visegar had a vast level of management running its many businesses. Each was run by an Alpha. They were normally powerful metas. Alpha reported to Tier 6 management, the lowest level of the upper management echelon. Rhys Polson and Ops reported to a Tier 5 manager. Mac had never met a Tier 4 or higher. So what was one doing here?

"PS assigned DJ and Rath as their primary protective operatives. The file says that they were also going to ask you and Cell to attend but Blindspot specifically requested Gunner as his primary guard. Knowing PS, they would not have been pleased with that."

"I'm guessing Gunner wasn't all that thrilled about it either," Mac mumbled. "Keep me updated. I still have work to do. Raven out."

Mac quietly approached the vehicle bay. It was a large warehouse building with doors big enough to park eighteen wheelers and their cargo. Mac crept to a smaller door and carefully opened it. She stepped inside, her eyes and rifle moving as one as they scanned the building. The first thing she saw was several large trucks and several pickups truck with large wheels. The second thing she saw was a bike that immediately made Mac fall in love.

It was a motorcycle.

Mac approached and found her heart beating faster as she crouched by it. It was a 1995 Ducati Super Sport 600 Scrambler that had been heavily customised. Whoever had built the bike had ditched the fairings and had swapped the original alloy wheels with spoked ones for a classic look. It also had received front dual disc brakes, knobby tyres and a custom leather seat, with bespoke British Competition Green paint gracing the fuel tank and black adorning the rest of the bike, including the custom frame. In that moment Mac wanted to ditch the mission, steal the bike and ride off with the power between her legs. Perhaps, when she saved the day, they'd give her the bike as a reward. That would be nice of them. It wasn't going to happen but it would still be nice.

Footsteps.

Mac snapped her head up and the rifle followed. From all around her she could hear footsteps and plenty of them. She caught glimpses of men running on the upper railings and heard others ducking behind cards and trucks. Just by sound alone she guessed there were nearly twenty people here. Each would be armed and each would be here to take her down. Somehow they knew she was coming. Somehow they had time to prepare. Mac swore. She had just walked into an ambush.

CHAPTER 06

Bailee stormed through the halls of Colville High School, anger flowing through her veins. When Bailee got mad, somebody got hurt and Bailee was *very* mad. Somebody was definitely going to get hurt and Bailee had one person in mind: Will Dennehy. She had given the police a chance to deal with this issue but they did nothing. Now it fell to her. Bailee pushed opened the boy's locker room and stormed in. The four teen jumped at Bailee's sudden and boisterous entrance.

"Call of nature?" Jack Galt - the wide receiver - asked. "It's in the back."

"Nah," Marshall Napier - the right guard - said. "She's probably one of those girls that cream for a footballer."

"You're Holly's friend?" Will Dennehy - quarterback - asked. "You want a taste of what she got?"

"I'll fucking kill you!" Bailee lost it. She stormed forward but was stopped by a man stepping before her, his arms held wide. Bailee looked at the red-headed teen. His name was Robert Millar.

"Whoa, what's going on? What is this about?" Millar asked.

"I slept with her BFF at the party last week and she's pissed 'cause she has a crush on me or some shit." Dennehy said. Will Dennehy was the star quarterback. He was tall, muscular and had raven black wavy hair. He was also a fucking asshole.

"You fucking raped her!" Bailee yelled. "She was drunk and she said no. You didn't care."

"She wanted it, she was all over me," Will laughed. "Now get lost."

When Gunner moved Bailee to Colville, she had difficulty making friends. Colville was the type of town where people either left as soon as they could or they died there. Family lines ran deep and most people had to do a family tree check before they dated anybody. Outsiders were rare and often didn't fit in. Holly Silverburgh was different. She found Bailee interesting and tried to get to know her. The two become fast friends.

Two weeks ago they were invited to a football team party. They were fifteen years old and were freshmen. The football team was made up of senior students, freshmen *never* got invited. So when the invitation came, Bailee and Holly jumped at the chance. They promised to keep an eye on each other but during the party they got separated. Bailee knew that Holly had a crush on Will. Colville was a football town and Colville High was on a winning season. This meant that *every* girl had a thing for Will. Bailee never doubted that Holly would wear her sexiest clothes and would try to make out with Will but Bailee also knew that Holly would never let it go any further, no matter how drunk she was.

"You did what?" Millar spun toward the quarterback. "You raped a fifteen year old? What the fuck is wrong with you?"

"I didn't rape her. The girl was *begging* for it. You didn't see how she came on to me. You didn't see what she was wearing." Will shook his head. "Are you really taking her side over your own teams?"

"I'll stand by this team for just about anything," Millar defended. "But you raped a girl. No means no, you sick fuck."

"Jesus, Millar," Galt shook his head. "No wonder you're warming the bench. You're a fucking bitch."

Bailee looked at Millar. Despite his ugly-ass red hair,

the guy was actually pretty cute. He had a very circular face with chiseled features. He looked like a ginger-Paul Walker. Bailee liked Paul Walker, especially topless in *Into the Blue*.

"What do you play?"

"I'm the backup QB."

"Not that he gets any field time with our champ here," Napier laughed, clapping Will on the shoulder.

"If you leave now, your life will get a whole hell of a lot better," Bailee said. She looked out across the room. "That goes for any of you. If you leave now, you won't get hurt. But if you stay, then you are just *begging* for what happens next."

Millar looked at Bailee and stepped aside. He had heard the rumours and he'd seen her run. She was a beast. The track team ran beside the football field. Occasionally, when the coach was feeling sadistic, he'd make the football team run alongside the track team. Bailee outran each and every guy on his team and often lapped them. She was a machine. Millar grabbed his jacket and exited by the locker room door. That left only three to deal with.

"Last chance," she offered. The Napier and Galt stepped forward. Bailee shrugged. She warned them.

Bailee let her anger fade as logic flowed through her. She needed her mind. Gunner had taught her that fighting was more than simply punching and kicking. A good fighter knew how to think in a fight. The difficult part was not to overthink. A fighter - a good fighter - had to be able to think, calculate and adjust all on a moment's notice. Bailee wasn't a good fighter but she was getting there.

Galt was on her left and Napier was on her right. Galt was the wide receiver. It was his job to run fast and catch a ball. Because of this he was tall and fit. Napier was the right guard. His job was to stop anybody from crossing the line of scrimmage. He was a massive bulk of muscles and strength. He was the fat farm boy who was really strong. Either of them outweighed her and together they easily outclassed her. Sadly, neither of them had a chance. Neither of them had been trained by Gunner.

Napier stepped forward and grabbed Bailee's right shoulder with his right hand. Thousands of hours of Gunner's training kicked in and she reacted. Bailee grabbed the hand by the wrist and twisted away from her. Her left foot shot out and struck Napier in his right knee; Bailee watched as the leg buckled. His entire center of gravity shifted leaving the teen off balance. Galt dashed in from the left. He wanted to save his friend but he never made it close. Bailee's left leg shot out and her running shoe covered foot slammed Galt in the chest. The receiver flew backwards. Back on both feet, Bailee shifted all of her weight and pushed to her right. The off balanced guard tried to find his footing but failed. Bailee pitched Napier to the side and watched as he toppled through several locker room benches, breaking many on the way down.

Bailee pivoted around just in time to Galt charge back at her. His right hand cocked as he prepared to punch her. For a brief moment Bailee was impressed that Galt was willing to fight her straight up. Most farm boys in Colville wouldn't raise their hand to hit a woman until they had been married to them for at least five years. The punch was obvious, he had telegraphed the move a mile away and Bailee had eons to react. She ducked under the fist and fired one of her own. She fired her left fist into his left thigh. Her fist retracted only to fire again, this time punching into the right side of his gut. Bailee stepped back and spun, her spinning kick colliding with Galt's chin and pitching him to the ground.

She heard footsteps and pivoted. A frightened Will was trying to escape. Bailee spun low with her legs and swept the QB's feet out from underneath him. He toppled to the locker room floor and fell hard. Bailee grabbed Will by his hand and twisted. He screamed.

"On your feet, asshole." Bailee pulled back until Will scrambled to his feet. Bailee slammed him chest first against the nearest wall, his arm still pinned by Bailee behind his back.

"What the fuck? What the fuck?" He screamed. "I'm sorry. I'm sorry."

"You were her first," Bailee said evenly. It was the calm that frightened Will even more. If she had been angry he could know what to expect. But this calm, Hannibal-esque as it was, was beyond frightening. "She was a virgin before that night. You took that from her. You robbed her of her innocence and you robbed her of her trust. She can never get either of those back. Now I have to take something from you, something you can never get back.

"This is your final year in high school football, right? This is the year that scouts show up and watch you play? Then this year is very important to you. This is the year that will either turn you pro or keep you stuck in this town for the rest of your life. With your winning streak scouts must be lining up to offer you a chance at their college." Will's eyes went wide with fear. His body began to shake. "I'm going to take that chance from you."

"No, no, no, God, no; please don't," Will begged. Bailee didn't listen. She lined up her foot and struck. Blow after blow connected with his right leg and knee until she heard the satisfying crack. Bailee released his arm and watched him fall. Will screamed in agony, tears rolling down his face. Bailee turned away and exited the locker room. Millar waited outside the room, pacing up and down the hallway. He paused and looked at her.

"What did you do?" he hesitantly asked.

"I got you off the bench," she said.

Gunner opened his front door and found Sheriff Brian Dennehy standing there with a deputy behind him. Sheriff Dennehy was a large man with a square jaw and grey cowboy hat that sat atop a head of hair that was once as raven black as his son's. Gunner didn't say a word. He just stood there, quietly eating an apple.

"Gunner, I need to come inside." Gunner took another bite as he shook his head. Dennehy sighed. "I need to arrest your daughter."

"What did she do?"

"Don't do this, Gunner. You and I are friends. I wouldn't do this if I had to but this is fucking serious."

"What did she do?" Gunner repeated, this time drawing out each word.

"She assaulted my boy. She broke his leg. He'll never play ball again." Dennehy sighed. "The town wants to tan her hide. She just ruined our chance at state and she just took away my boy's future. I can't look the other way on this one."

"But you can look the other way when you son rapes a fifteen year-old?" Gunner asked.

"Fuck sakes, Gun. It was a high school party. They were all drunk and kids are saying she was throwing herself at him. What am I supposed to do? There were no witnesses in the bedroom so it's a *he said she said* thing. Am I supposed to ruin my boy's future at the NFL over some girl's claim that nobody can prove?"

"You are supposed to do your fucking job, Brian. I know he's the star quarterback. I know he's your son but he's also assaulted a girl. Your son is a fucking rapist and you looked the other way." Gunner pointed to the star on his chest. "If you can't do the job, then lose the star."

"I'm going to do my fucking job," the Sheriff said, visibly angry now. "You daughter assaulted my boy. I have two witnesses saying she also assaulted them."

"Your boy's goons? They would say anything to back him up. To me this sounds like a *he said she said* thing."

"Damn it, Gunner. I'm coming into this house and I'm arresting your daughter for assault."

"You can try but you'll never make it past me," Gunner promised. "If you want to go to war with me, then have at it but know that I will rain fucking hell down upon you. It will be a scorched earth scenario by the time I'm done. I will fucking destroy you before you lay a finger on my daughter." The two men silently stared at each other. "Your boy fucked up and he paid the price. None of this would have happened if you did your job as a cop or as a parent."

Mac was surrounded. She could see Russian men above her on the upper walkways and peeking out from behind cover. She knew she was surrounded and each of them had a gun trained on her. Mac's mind raced. She needed to think and she had to do it quickly.

"I have waited a long time for us to meet. I have parted the seas and I have shifted the lands for us to meet." The female soldier emerged from a second floor office stood atop the upper walkway. She looked down with an arrogant smirk on her face. Yet the moment her eyes fell upon Mac, the smirk vanished and was replaced with surprise. "Holy shit, you're a girl."

"You sure," Mac mocked. "Maybe you should take a closer look."

"Is that an offer?"

"Cute," Mac glared. "Who the hell are you?"

"I am Major Renata Shatalov and you were not who I was expecting."

"I rarely am." Her mind raced as she thought about her options. There was the door behind her, the one she came in from, but during Shatalov's speech she heard the sound of thumping and scraping along the wall. It meant there were soldiers outside that door waiting for her and that the soldiers were hugging the wall for cover; rookie mistake. She needed to stall. "This is your only chance, walk away and you won't get hurt."

"My men have you outnumbered," Shatalov laughed. "The odds aren't really in your favour."

"Then play those odds and see what happens."

"I like you. I was expecting somebody else but I'm glad we ---" Mac cut off her words with a squeeze of her trigger. With her M4 aimed at the walkway, she fired three burst of three. The rounds flew across the hanger and slammed against the covered railing. The shots weren't meant to kill, they were meant cause panic. The soldiers above her ducked for cover as the frightening sound of bullets ricocheting off of metal occurred mere feet away from them. Mac lowered her weapon and fired a pair of rounds at three nearby trucks, forcing the soldiers to duck back behind them as cover. Then Mac ran.

She spun around and fired three single rounds against the back wall. Screams of surprise emerged from the other side of the wall. Mac ducked behind a truck and crouched down. She ejected the mag and replaced it with a fresh one. Mac peered around the corner of the truck and saw a group of three approaching from her left. She peered around the other corner and saw two more coming from her right. Mac needed to shift the balance. She reached into her bag and withdrew a grenade. She only had two so she had to use them wisely. She pulled the pin and slid it along the ground behind her. The grenade slid along the ground, beneath a truck until it emerged on the other side. Seconds later it exploded. Mac popped up around the right corner and opened fire. Two rounds into one soldier and two into a second. Both dropped. Mac pivoted to her left just in time to see the trio approach from the left.

Mac used the tip of her M4 barrel like a bayonet and slapped the enemy rifle away from her. She thrust again and stabbed the soldier in the neck. He coughed for air but never got the chance to gain any. Mac smashed the soldier across the face with the butt of her rifle. The first soldier dropped and Mac pivoted to the second. She jabbed at the man with her rifle twice, one in the chest and once under his arm. After the second jab she sidestepped and twisted, trapping the arm with her rifle and pinning it behind the soldier's back. The third soldier looked at her, a pistol in his hand and an unsure look on his face. Mac spun the trapped soldier into the side of the truck and watched as the impact knocked him out. She dropped her rifle, letting the sling catch it, and lunged for the third soldiers. Her hands moved quickly. Her left grabbed the weapon and pushed it away while her right struck thrice, first in the chest, second in the neck and third in the face. Then she grabbed his arm with both hands and flipped him over her shoulder. The soldier crashed to the cement floor with a heavy thud. Mac ducked back behind the truck. She stole a quick glance at the stolen handgun that resided in her grip and frowned. It wasn't a Serdyukov SR1 or a MP-443 Grach. It was a SIG Sauer P226. Her hunch was getting stronger. She pocketed the weapon and took her rifle back in both hands. She still had a fight to win.

She popped out of cover and opened fire once more. She fired at the raised platform and watched as her first round ripped through the skull of an unsuspecting soldier. Any hesitation she had about killing had vanished the moment they opened fire on her. Killing a sentry was one thing, killing a soldier who had just ambushed her was another. Her rate of fire was steady and her aim was exact. Shot after shot rang out from her rifle as round after round found a new home. Not all shots were kill shots, some were leg or arm shots, but they were enough to take them out of combat and leave her alive.

Mac spotted a second door to the far side and bolted for it. She grabbed her final grenade, pulled the pin and lobbed it at the door she had entered from. She hears scream of panic and then an explosion. That would stop any from trying to follow her. Mac exited the hanger and bolted for the tree line. Seconds later she vanished from view, hidden once more in the cover of nature provided by Tongass National Forest.

CHAPTER 07

Bailee leaned into Robert Millar's strong arms and simply let herself melt. There was something about being in his arms that brought out a different side in her. When she was with him she wasn't the super soldier that Gunner was training. She was simply a fifteen year-old girl who was watching a movie with her boyfriend. When she was with him she could simply be normal.

They cuddled on her couch deep in Bailee's living room, watching some dumb movie they'd seen a dozen times before. It was the early days of summer. School had just ended and summer was underway. Bailee turned in Millar's arms and lean in to kiss him. The pair's lips met and for moment there was nothing but heavenly bliss.

"So when are you going to mention whatever it is you want to talk about?" Bailee asked.

"I...I...what are you talking about?" Millar stammered.

"You're horrible at this," Bailee mocked. She climbed out of Millar's arms and looked at him directly. "You've been trying to build up the nerve to talk to me since you got here. So why don't you just say it."

"I...I..."

"You want to break up," Bailee suggested.

"No, wait, I mean..." Millar sighed. "How did you know?"

"The Old Man has been teaching me lots of things," Bailee began. "One of which is how to notice things. It's more than simply *seeing* things. You have to know how to notice and process them.

"You've been distant and less affectionate. You've been squirmy since we sat down and your hands have been less...." She fought a smile. "They've kept to themselves lately. It's kinda been disappointing that way."

Millar let out small smile. She never failed to impress him. Bailee was unlike any girl in the school. She was unlike any girl he'd met. Bailee was strong and tough. She saw things that others didn't and she viewed the world differently. The pair had been dating for almost six months. Millar nervously asked her out two weeks after the locker room incident. She had sheepishly said yes.

"My dad taught me how to hunt and play ball," Millar said. "Yours teaches you so much differently. The world could end tomorrow and you would be okay because of what he taught you."

"The Old Man is weird that way," Bailee lied. She knew the truth behind his teaching. She also knew what confidential meant.

"Why do you never call him your father?"

"For the same reason he never calls me his daughter. Titles are different when you're adopted and relationships are different after you've lost someone. The Old Man and I have each lost a lot." Bailee tapped Millar in the chest. "You, however, are changing the subject off of our break up."

"I don't *want* to break up but I think we should," Millar said. "I'm leaving for Florida State in the fall and you still have two years left of school."

"And you want to fuck college girls."

"No!" Bailee jokingly elbowed him. He rolled his eyes. "It's the distance and it's also the age gap. I..." His words trailed off. Bailee prodded him for more. With a sigh Millar continued. "I don't want you putting your life on hold for me. I don't know if I'm ever coming back to this town. I want you to live your life."

"Is this it?" Bailee asked. "Is this our last date?"

"I don't know."

"Do you want to date the rest of the summer and end it in the fall?" She suggested. Millar nodded. Bailee straddled Millar and began unbuttoning his shirt. "Since I'm now on a limited timeline with you and since we've got the house to ourselves, I think I need to make the most of our time together."

Millar smiled and kissed her again.

Bailee heard the front door slam. She looked up from the TV and spotted Gunner entering the house. Millar had long since left. She eyed the Old Man and studied his face. Gunner was never one to overly emote but if one looked, they could see the signs of distress on his face.

"You okay?" she asked.

"Nope." Gunner looked at her and frowned. With a single look he could see Bailee was hurting as well. "What happened?"

"Robert put a clock on our relationship. Come fall, it is over."

"You okay with that?" Gunner asked. He kicked off his boots and sat down beside her. Bailee just shrugged.

"I knew it was coming. He's two years older than me, he's a football star and he's just been recruited by a Division 1 football school. I knew this wasn't going to last into next year."

"It still hurts, don't it?" Bailee nodded. Gunner put his arm around her and pulled her close. "I'm sorry, Kiddo. I know this must be tough. Ending it with your first can be hard."

"How did you...." Bailee began to ask but her words trailed off. She decided against it. Gunner simply always knew. "What happened with you?"

"Tina called it quits." Tina was a woman that Gunner had been dating. She was also the librarian at Colville High School. "She says I am too distant for her. She thinks I have too many walls that prevent her from getting to know me."

"Did you tell her about the super-powered bad guys you fight? That would probably win her over."

"That's a big secret to dump," Gunner said, "although a secret like that could also keep a quarterback in state."

Bailee elbowed the old man and he laughed. The pair rested in each other's arms, each using the other as quiet support and comfort. Gunner leaned down and kissed Bailee's forehead. "Wanna shoot shit until we feel better?"

"I was wondering how much longer I had to cuddle before I could suggest that," Bailee replied. "I mean, I know how important cuddling is to someone like you."

"Some days you're more of a guy then I am," Gunner mocked.

"And some days you're more of a girl then I am," Bailee laughed as she climbed to her feet. "Did you at least get break up sex with my school's naughty librarian?"

"I'm not having this conversation with you, Kiddo," Gunner said as followed.

"I ask 'cause *I got* break up sex with Robert."

"You know when I said *shoot shit* I didn't mean targets," Gunner snarled. "I meant shooting the footballer who dares to touch my girl."

"Can it wait until the fall?" Bailee asked in a teasing tone. "I'd like to have plenty more break up sex between now and then."

"You're grounded, Kiddo," Gunner yelled. "You're grounded until your thirty."

Mac crouched by a tree. She fought to steady her breathing and calm her heart. This was far from her first gunfight but it didn't matter. Each time she fought and each time she shot, her heart raced. Mac kept her rifle up as she scanned the trees. Her gaze never dropped until she was certain she was alone.

Mac dropped to the ground with a plop and let out an exhausted sigh. How the hell was she ambushed? There was no way for them to know she was going to head to the vehicle bay. Even if someone had seen her walk towards it, there was no way they could have organized that many troops to be waiting for her. Her mind raced. She had to focus on the details. Gunner had always taught her that this job was less about fighting and killing, it was about noticing the details that others missed and piecing together the puzzle. That's what she had to do now. There was so much about this mission that didn't make sense.

Why did the Russians attack the base?

The cover story was that a splinter cell of the Russian Ground Forces needed meta-support. This left many unanswered questions. Why did they attack Morrell Blood? This base wasn't rich with meta-tech or powered humans. This base wasn't even on the map of most valuable targets. This led to a second question. How did they even know about Morrell Blood? Mac had a high clearance within Visegar but even she hadn't heard about the base until earlier today. Mac knew there was lots about Visegar she was kept in the dark about but if this was as secretive as Keane was letting on, then how did General Petrov and Major Shatalov know about it? This also brought up a question about the soldiers themselves. Some of them walked and talked like Russians but others did not. Others used non-RGF weapons. Mac pulled free the stolen pistol from her bag. She ejected the mag and cleared the chamber. She turned the pistol around in her hand as she inspected it.

It was a SIG Sauer P226. It feature SIGLITE front and rear night sights, an integral Picatinny rail, black anodized frame and Nitron-coated stainless steel slide. It had a slightly longer barrel length then a normal P266 and also had external threads, both of which were designed to accept a suppressor. Mac glanced at the logo etched onto the weapon's slide and wooden grips. Staring back at her was a white star encompassed in a circle. This was the unmistakable logo for WhiteStar Security.

Mac cursed.

WhiteStar was a private military company that had government contracts for both overseas and at home. They were one of the largest PMCs in the world and even had a contract to run and operate the Center for Disease Control's fast response ADVERT team. They were also owned by Polaris Industries. Mac had dealt with WhiteStar dozens of times. Most of them were thugs who liked to kill. The worst part was that they were *highly trained* thugs who liked to kill.

If these were not Russians and were instead actually WhiteStar agents, then some of Mac's questions were answered. It did, however, create all new ones. Polaris and Visegar had been at war for generations. The two hidden companies constantly battled each other in corporate espionage and outright combat. WhiteStar was even involved in a scandal involving kidnapped children. Spin doctors turned the entire event into a collection of *former WhiteStar employees* in an effort to save the company. Regardless of who attacked the base, the question still remained.

Why did they attack the base?

"*Trautman*: come in."

"We read you, Raven. Go for *Trautman*." It was Keane's voice.

"Do you have any update on the electrical meta?"

"Negative, Raven."

"Nothing?"

"Nothing certain."

"Give me what you got."

"I'd advise against that, Raven. False information could lead to poor decisions in the field," Ford replied.

"Give me what you've got," Mac said while rolling

her eyes. "I'll figure things out as we go."

"The image wasn't a good one. Our systems give us a thirty-nine percent match with one Aedan Orman," Ford recited. "He is an electrical meta who used to be a member of the Real IRA."

Mac sighed. The Real Irish Republic Army; that was just freaking great. Mac hated dealing with the IRA, Provisional or not. They were always a pain in her fucking ass. The Provisional Irish Republican Army was an Irish republican paramilitary organization that sought to remove Northern Ireland from the United Kingdom and to bring about an independent socialist republic encompassing all of Ireland. They formed in 1969 and did some real nasty shit until they negotiated a ceasefire in 1997. The Real Irish Republic Army was a group that splintered off from the Provisional. The Real IRA was made up of dissident members who rejected the ceasefire. According to the United Kingdom and the United States, the Real IRA was a terrorist organization.

"Orman and his sister, Einin Moran, nee Orman, are in their forties. Orman joined the IRA when he was a teenager but Einin wanted nothing to do with it. Orman participated in several attacks during the 90s. Einin went and got married at a young age to one Liam Moran and had one child together.

"During an SAS raid, Aedan and several other IRA members were grabbed. A gunfight broke out and Liam Moran was killed. Einin joined the IRA and helped to free her brother. Since then the two have been active members in the fight. When the Real IRA splintered off, the two followed, continuing the fight.

"In April and May of 2015, the sibling duo led two bomb attacks in Derry, Ireland. They bombed the offices of the probation board and had two partially exploded bombs at the perimeter fence of the British Army Reserve Base.

"In the Reserve Base bombing something went wrong. One of the bombs detonated early and killed twenty-two Real IRA members and nearly killed the siblings. The pair survived by the activation of the Lycotta gene. Because they were the only ones to survive, the pair were blamed and called British collaborators. They were hunted by both SAS and Real IRA member. They were forced to flee. If they ever set foot in Ireland, they'll both be shot or arrested."

"So why didn't you want to tell me this?" Mac asked.

"Because our tracking data doesn't match with this situation. Last we have of them is working with WhiteStar in exchange for asylum."

And there it was, the confirmation she needed. Mac looked down at the P226 WhiteStar Tactical pistol and sighed. Part of her was hoping that they weren't WhiteStar and actually were Russians but fate was never that kind. The vermin that were WhiteStar were once again messing with her life.

"I have found WhiteStar equipment on some of the soldiers," Mac reluctantly added. "I think this is a WhiteStar attack."

Silence.

"Confirm that, Raven."

"I repeat, I think this is a WhiteStar attack."

"Fuck."

"Roger that," Mac said. "I have another name for you to look up. She is the troop commander for this mission. Her name is Major Renata Shatalov."

"We'll look into it, Raven. *Trautman* out."

CHAPTER 08

Bailee sat by the small fire and tried to keep a neutral look on her face. As much as she enjoyed camping with Gunner - a fact that had surprised a city girl like herself - what she hated was dealing with Gunner's friends. None scared her more than the masked man named Rath.

Rath was a tall man, standing just less than six feet tall. He was a well built man with more muscles then Bailee had ever seen. His stature was intimidating but that wasn't what scared her the most. Her fear came from the mask that Rath wore. Rath always wore a black hood with large white eyes.

"So this is the girl you've told me about," Rath said as he sat down by the fire. Bailee was twelve and this was the first time she had ever met the large man.

"Yeah," Gunner said as he handed Rath a beer. The man lifted his mask above his lips. "This is Bailee MacIntosh."

"Mic-Intosh?" Rath asked as he took a sip.

"*Mac*-Intosh," Bailee quickly corrected.

Rath snickered. He looked at Gunner. "I never pictured you as a dad and definitely never pictured you with a daughter."

Bailee and Gunner silently eyed each other for a moment before Gunner shook his head. "It's not like that. We're just...." Gunner's words trailed off.

"We're just looking after each other," Bailee finished. Rath just smiled. He'd known Gunner for a while and he was happy that the man had found someone. He never suspected that it would be a kid.

"So what do we want to talk about?"

"Subtle," Gunner mocked. He saw through Rath's thinly veil question. "She knows of my work."

"Wait, are you training her?" Rath asked. Gunner just nodded. Rath shook her head. "Don't force her into this world, Gunner."

"I'm not," Gunner said, stealing glances at Bailee. "It's not like that. I'm just training her. It's her choice what she does with the skills I've given her."

Rath eyed the pair but eventually just shrugged. He took another swig of beer. For several moments the three of them sat in silence, the two men drinking. Eventually Rath spoke.

"When I was younger - almost twenty years ago," Rath paused at the number and shook his head. He restarted his story. "When I was younger I was kind of famous. It made things difficult when my super strength suddenly appeared."

"You sure about this, Rath?" The muscle-man nodded.

"Powers are difficult to control, especially in the beginning. My strength's arrival came with blood. I brought down a small building and accidently hurt people." Rath took a deep breath. It was clear of the pain he still felt. "Visegar intervened; they are the only reason I'm not in jail. They kept my story quiet in exchange for my assistance. My face is still memorable, so when I work with Visegar I'm forced to wear the mask or a disguise."

Rath pulled off his mask. Bailee's eyes went wide. She knew *that* face. She recognized *that* face. Most of the world would have recognized *that* face. Bailee pointed and opened her mouth to speak.

"We don't say his name," Gunner quickly interrupted. "We're not allowed to say his name. That is why we call him

Rath."

Bailee stood there, stunned. For several moments she searched for something to say, for *anything* to say. Eventually words came. "I thought you said you were only *kind of* famous?"

Rath laughed. "Welcome to the secret, Mac."

Bailee blushed. "It's Bailee. I don't like being called Mac."

Mac circled around the base, moving exceptionally slowly. Soldiers were everywhere and they were doing their best to find her. Mac was doing her best to make them failures. Mac needed to get eyes on the dorms. She suspected that the hostages were being held there. If Rath or DJ were there, then she could possibly free them and finally have some backup.

Mac hid amongst the tree and withdrew her binoculars. She stared down as the dorm's door opened. Mac watched as several armed guards pulled Rath out of the building. Mac pocketed her binoculars and she gripped her rifle. This was her chance. Mac quickly slid down the hill. She slid to a halt and raised her rifle. There were five guards. She could make five quick shots, free Rath and both could escape to the trees and regroup.

Mac readied her first shot. She knew Rath wouldn't miss an opportunity like this to escape. With a burst of strength, Rath snapped his cuffs and backhanded the nearest guard. The soldier went flying backwards into the air. Mac lined up a shot but stopped when a humming sound suddenly filled the air. Mac quickly scanned the area but saw nothing. Two seconds later, the humming got louder and a blurry purple form slammed into Rath. The masked man slammed into the side of the dorms. Rath climbed back to his feet and prepared to fight whatever it was that hit him. The blur slammed him again. The blur came to a halt as the form of a woman came into view. She was a dark-skinned woman dressed in black pants, a red shirt and a brown Bolero jacket. She wore her hair in a bob-style haircut. The hair started black at the top but the further it fell the more it changed until it was a violet colour.

Mac swore. She backed away. That woman was a speedster and they were always trouble. They could dodge bullets, move faster than the eye could follow and some could even break the sound barrier. There was no way to win a straight up fight. Mac needed to deal with the speedster in another way. She reluctantly watched as the soldiers grabbed her masked friend by his arms and started to drag him across the base. She was so close.

Einin Moran felt her brother approach before she heard or saw him. She could see anybody in the forest, she could feel what the trees felt and be one with nature. For a city girl like herself, one that *hated* nature, it was an ironic *gift* of a power. Yet despite her abilities, it wasn't hard to find Aeden Orman. Nature didn't like her brother, to the trees he felt wrong.

"Dryad," Aeden said.

"I hate that name, brother," she sighed, not looking at him. "It is a silly name. At least they named you after a thunder god."

"I don't know," Aeden said with a shrug. "Taranis doesn't roll off the tongue."

"What do you want to be called? Green Lightning? Bolt? Zapdos?"

"That last one is a Pokémon," he grumbled, ashamed that he knew that. "Do you have her again?"

"She's easy to track in the trees." Aeden gave his sister a raised eyebrow. "Maybe not *easy* but *easier* perhaps? I don't know how she does it. I should be able to follow anything foreign in the trees but she is nearly impossible to track." Aeden nodded slowly. He wasn't agreeing to anything in particular that she was saying, he was just nodding as he fell deep in thought.

"Ever since she recruited us," Einin spoke, "Shatalov has been right about a lot. She's good at predicting how things will play out."

"She's kept us alive," Aeden said. "That's about enough for me."

"But she didn't predict her," Einin said, nodding to the woods while ignoring her brother's simplistic thoughts. "She said we'd be facing off against Thanatos."

"She talks so much about this guy," Aeden said apathetically. "It's her boogie man. I ain't the type to be afraid of boogie men, especially ones that ain't here. Now, I'm gonna go down there, find this girl and do as we've been ordered to." Aden held up a ball of lightning and a sinister grin. "I'm gonna zap her."

"Raven, this is Zetes, Do you copy?" Mac dropped to one knee.

"Go for Raven," Mac replied to her radio. Mac smiled. "I am happy to hear your voice, Zetes. What's your location?"

"I'm at Home Base. I can't get there in time to provide any physical assistance but you have me here on the radio. Whatever you need, Boss Lady, I'm here."

"Have they kept you up-to date?"

"Yep."

"Good." Mac chose her next words carefully. "I need a favour from you, like you gave me back in Prague."

Mac's team was built entirely from meta humans. Aside from Rath, she knew little of each before their files came across her desk. They were now some of the few souls in the world she trusted. Rath, DJ, Cell and Zetes; she trusted each of these men with her life. She had rode into hell with each of them and climbed back out. Mac had always had issues with emotions, an issue not uncommon with orphaned children, but she loved these men. They were her boys and each of them knew it. Their shared experiences made it so they could talk volumes with few words. So when Mac mentioned Prague, Zetes knew exactly what she meant.

Jasper 'Zetes' Hill was an elemental meta. He had the power to create and control wind. Mac had recruited him from - of all places - the US Coast Guard. He was a sailor who had developed his powers when he was ten years old. Jasper was using the coast guard to fund a smuggling operation. Along with being a natural meta, Jasper was also a natural face. He could talk and charm his way into anything. Mac met Jasper when his operation went belly up and he was unable to talk his way out of it.

In the three years since she joined his team, Zetes had proven a quick thinker and a useful member, especially in Prague. Four months after joining, Mac's team was assigned to act as security for a Prague lab. Shortly after the mission began nearly every person in a six block radius was suddenly filled with a blind murderous rage and an urge to storm the Visegar lab. Mac and he team did everything they could to protect the building while keeping the death count low. It wasn't until Cell and DJ began digging into the building's secrets that they discovered the lab was performing an amplification test on a young psychic. The unexpected effect was the angry psychic had pushed his rage on anybody in range. Mac and Zetes were able to end the experiment and quell the psionic rage. Since that day, mentioning Prague was a code that they needed to *covertly* investigate the building in question. In this case Mac had just asked Zetes to use any contacts he had to figure out what secrets Morrell Blood was hiding.

"I understand, Raven. What do you need?"

"I need you to..." Mac's words were cut off as she felt every hair on her body stand on end. Even the hairs on her head began to float upwards. Mac pivoted around, worried as to what the cause was, but didn't have a chance to react as a blast of lightning slammed into her chest and pitched her backwards into the air. Mac's body stiffened as she crashed into the dirt. For a moment Mac was still. She had lost all motor skill. She tried to move but her body didn't respond. She was awake and cognizant of everything was happening but that only made it worse. Mac began to panic. She wanted to scream for help but nothing came. She couldn't even make a sound. She was a woman trapped in her own broken body. Memories flooded her mind, memories of being pinned and trapped in the wreckage of her parent's car crash. Memories of not being able to move and not being able to save herself or her parents assaulted her mind.

As quickly as it vanished, control of her body returned and the first words from her lips were a loud and boisterous fuck. Her hands moved on instinct and quickly gripped her rifle. Mac scanned the horizon as she looked for the bolt's source but he was nowhere to be seen.

"Move," Mac ordered herself. "Get off the fucking ground and get back on your feet."

Mac obeyed her orders and scrambled to her feet. It was an awkward scramble, Mac never wanting to let go of her weapon, but eventually she was back on both feet. She just stood there.

"Cover; find cover."

Mac blinked twice before dashing behind the nearest tree. She crouched behind the large western red cedar tree. She did a quick check of her body. Her fingers tingled, her body hurt and she could smell the sickening scent of burning hair but she was okay. Mac took several deep breaths as she tried to calm her panic. Aeden Orman had hit her with a long range blast of lightning. The blast had the same effect as taser gun did. Tasers were designed for neuromuscular incapacitation. They were built to deliver an electric charge that interfered with its target's peripheral nervous system, creating uncontrollable muscular convulsions and rendering them temporarily unable to control their own movements. Mac repeated the clinical terms in her head to lessen the fright she had from that blast. Mac was afraid of very little but being stuck in a broken body? It was enough to keep her awake at night.

"Where did ya go, lass?" Aeden Irish accent carried through the trees. It was thick and full of distress, like his voice had become raspy and hoarse due to a life of regret and conflict."Why don't ya step out so I can see yer pretty eyes?"

A second blast slammed the ground where Mac once lay. She let out a small yelp and her heart raced again. In a panic filled move, Mac bolted from her tree and dashed for another. She slid behind another cedar. Her chest rapidly heaved as breathing became hard. Mac fought for air.

"Raven, come in," Zetes voice cried out over the radio. The signal was static filled, a result of the lightning being tossed around, but she could still make out his words. "Are you okay, Raven?"

"I got hit, Zetes," Mac replied. "It wasn't bad but it--"

A third blast slammed into Mac's tree. The bolt splintered some of the bark and caused a loud crack. Mac let out a yelp. She leaned out of cover and snapped off a pair of rounds. She didn't know where she was aiming but it felt like the thing to do.

"Raven, you need to focus!" Zetes cried out through the radio. The wind user sat at base, hundreds of miles away, slamming his fist into the desk. He needed to be there, he needed to help her but he couldn't. He was stuck on radio duty. Zetes roared and with a gust of wind tossed a nearby desk across the room. He was *not* good at desk duty. "Listen to me, Raven. I know what you've been through and I know what ticks your fear boxes but this ain't it. This ain't some paralyzing car crash or some random bullet to the spine. This is some asshole with powers. You can't fight a car crash but you can fight some bully who can make electricity. I mean fuck, my portable cell phone charger can create electricity and it has a god damned flashlight on it. Does this guy have a flashlight?"

Zetes words brought a small chuckle to her lips and

a small chuckle was all it took. Laughter broke through the panic and calm and training began to set in. She needed to keep her cool and keep her head in the game. She was never going to get a decent shot off if her hands were shaking.

"I'm good. Thank you, Zetes," Mac said as she readied herself.

"Now take this fucking battery pack down."

Aeden watched the cedar closely. He knew she was behind there; he just had to wait until she popped her head out again. Her last attempt to pop out resulted in two wildly fired shots. This time he was going to drop her. He stared forward at the tree but a glimmer to his left caught his eye. He turned his head around just in time to see the woman, in the distance, aim her rifle directly at him. He pivoted to the side, ducking behind a tree of his own, as two rounds passed by and narrowly missed him. How the fuck did she do that? How did she move without him seeing?

Einin voice filled his ear. "She's moving again. She's moving to your 9 o'clock. Fuck, she's hard to track."

Aeden popped out and fired a blast. It wasn't a charged bolt; those took a few seconds to build up. It was a bolt more akin to sticking a fork in an electrical socket. The blast slammed into the ground and left a divot but it did not hit the woman.

"Where is she?"

"I...I don't know. I can't find her."

"Keep searching." Aeden kept his eyes peeled. He couldn't see her and that scared the Irishman. He looked out over the trees. If he couldn't see her, maybe he could draw her out. "The boss told us to expect someone. She didn't tell us to expect you."

Mac popped out and fired another pair of rounds. Aeden dove out of the way. He returned with a medium bolt but the lightning collided only with a tree.

"People have been saying that to me all day," Mac yelled out. She ejected her mag and reloaded her rifle. She wasn't going to be in her current spot long, so she didn't mind revealing her position especially if there was a chance to get more intel. "Just who the hell have you been expecting?"

"We've been expecting the boogeyman, lass." Aeden's hands moved quickly as he formed a large ball of lightning between his palms. "We don't know his name. Shatalov simply calls him Thanatos."

Aeden popped out from his tree and fired his charged blast. The ball ripped through the tree Mac was using as cover, exploding through the trunk and sending splinters everywhere, but Mac was already gone.

"Location?" he asked into his radio.

"I don't know," Einin frantically replied. "7 o'clock!"

Aeden pivoted and fired. It was a pair of quick blast that slammed into the side of a sprinting Mac. The first caused her legs to stumble and the second knocked her off her feet. Mac hit the dirt hard. She lay there, unmoving, for a second. She feared what would happen if she called upon her body to move. Would it respond? Mac did her best to push away her panic and called upon her legs to move.

Move your legs, she thought.

Her legs moved. Mac sighed in relief as she rolled onto her back. She gripped her M4 and raised it, firing two bursts of three rounds. Both burst were aimed directly at the Irishman's chest.

Aeden raised his palms and force lightning outwards. It wasn't a blast; instead it was more of an outwards burst that pushed the bullets away from him. The rounds harmless passed on either side of him. He smirked at the girl.

"Is that all ye got, lass?" Aeden mocked.

Mac flipped to her feet and snapped her M4 up. She lined up her red holographic reticle onto Aeden's chest and began rapidly squeezing the trigger. Shot after shot ripped from her weapon's barrel. Each round tore through the air as they tried to rip into Aeden's chest but none succeeded. With an electrical burst, Aeden pushed each round away. Mac started firing her rounds slowly but with each passing second, her speed increased until the pause between each bang seemed to vanish complexly. Memories of the literal *thousands* of hours she'd spent training with Gunner flashed before and Mac couldn't help but smile. Aeden's struggled to keep the rounds away, the speed of his bursts increasing to meet her gun fire. Aeden knew what she was doing: she was trying to overwhelm him. She was trying to push him to his breaking point. It wasn't going to work. He had more electricity then she had bullets. The moment she had to reload was the moment he dumped so much electricity into her chest. All he had to do was wait.

Pain.

A sudden tearing pain emerged from Aeden's right leg. The Irishman fell to the ground, shocked. He glanced down and saw a gunshot wound in his right thigh. How? How did she do that? Aeden snapped his head back in her direction and raised both hands. Each palm quivered as a massive bolt of electricity emerged from them. He was trying to hit the woman with a final electrical blast but she was nowhere to be seen. Aeden crawled to a nearby tree.

"Where is she?"

"I don't know."

"Fucking find her!" Aeden screamed. He looked down at his wound and finally understood what had happened. The girl wasn't trying to overwhelm him; she was trying to distract him. It was magic 101. Get your target to look at the right hand while the left does all the work. He was so focused on deflecting all the rounds aimed at his chest that he didn't notice the one she shot at his leg.

"I can't find her," a panic stricken Einin said over the radio. "I don't know where she is. I can-- behind you!!"

Aeden spun his head behind and saw Mac standing there with a pistol in her hand. He raised his hand to fire but she snapped off a round into his shoulder. Aeden grunted loudly - ever the man - as his hand dropped to dirt, the electricity vanishing into the dirt.

"Wh...who are you?" Aeden asked.

"I'm Mac," she answered simply. "Why did you take the base?" Mac didn't yell or shout, she just spoke firmly and calmly and yet somehow they all still feared her.

"This is some fucking revenge mission," Aeden winced. "Shatalov wants revenge on her boogeyman."

"Don't bullshit me," Mac warned.

"I ain't. She wan--" Mac fired a second round from her silenced M17 and put a bullet into his left thigh. Aeden grunted again. "Boss Lady wants some stupid lab experiment. It's called the Nestor Ooze or some shite like that."

"Thank you," Mac replied.

"So what happens now, lass?" Aeden asked.

"You have three gunshot wounds. You're bleeding out. You won't make it back to base," Mac explained. "Your choices are to bleed out and die or I can end it here and stop the suffering."

"Can I have a final smoke?" Mac nodded. Aeden fished a cigarette and black lighter from his jacket pocket. He placed the cig between his lips. With a flick of the Zippo, he produced a small flame and lit the cig. With a second flick, the flame vanished. Aeden held up the Zippo. It was black with the image of a Smith & Wesson Model 29 .44 Magnum revolver on the side.

"Pa used to collect lighters and Zippos." Aeden scoffed at his own words but a smile formed across his lips. He took a puff and looked up at Mac. Her face remained stern and firm, the M17 still aimed down at his face. Aeden ignored the weapon and kept talking. "They be a stupid thing to collect but he enjoyed it. This one was from a movie called *The Dead Pool*. The only thing Pa loved more than a lighter was Dirty Harry. He mailed away for this one and waited eagerly for three weeks for it to arrive. The day it did, he went into Belfast to get it. On his way home he was shot and killed by British men. My Pa wasn't a fighter or a terrorist. He was factory worker who punched a clock everyday to feed his family. He just had the unlucky chance of being on that street when British men were fighting Irishmen. That was the day I decided to join the IRA. I decided to join so no honest father would ever die again because of the fucking British oppression."

Aeden tossed the lighter up to Mac. She swiftly snatched it out of the air. She gave it a cursory glance before looking back at him. Aeden smiled.

"Have it, lass," he said. "Every time you look at it remember that no matter how righteous your cause is somebody will always think you the villain." Aeden took a final puff of his cigarette and extinguished the butt in the dirt. He looked up and locked eyes with Mac. He took a deep breath and gave her a nod. Mac lined her pistol up with his forehead. With a cocky Irish smile, he spoke his final words. "Fuck the British."

Mac pulled the trigger.
Aeden Orman was dead.

CHAPTER 09

Einin Moran screamed as she felt her brother's life fade away. That woman had murdered her brother and left his soul for the trees. Einin dropped to the ground, tears pouring from her face. Einin was now alone and it was *that* woman's fault. It was all the fault of Mac.

She cried for several moments, her mind filled with rage and sorrow. She would never see her brother again, she would never hear him speak and she would never stop until she took her revenge, she would never stop until she killed this Mac.

Einin forced herself to her feet. Shatalov needed to know what had happened. She needed an update. The Irish woman forced one foot before the other. She repeated the process again and again until she was walking. She didn't know how or where she found the strength but she kept walking. She had to find Shatalov.

Mac knelt by Aeden's corpse. She search ever pocket on the body and pulled free what she could. Mac found a radio, a SIG Sauer P226 pistol, a folded piece of paper, a pack of smokes, a combat knife, a cell phone and a handful of coins. Mac picked up the radio. It was similar to the ones she saw before. It had a numerical pad that allowed certain codes to be entered. Depending on the code, a certain decryption process would activate allowed the two speakers to talk clearly. Simply put, only two people with the same proper codes could talk. Mac grabbed the paper and unfolded it. Just as she suspected, there were several codes.

- 14015
- 14112
- 14180
- 14025

Mac pocketed the paper. She inspected the phone but found it locked. She had hoped for a biometric lock but it was a six-digit code. She shrugged and dropped the phone on the ground. She didn't have time to figure it out. Mac swore. She hoped to find information as to why they were hunting Thanatos. She knew the name, most people in her world did. Thanatos was a Visegar operative that was known to leave a trail of bodies behind him. If you called upon Thanatos, there was going to be a body count. Most thought he was just an urban legend. Mac knew the truth. She knew Death's real name but she only ever called him *Old Man*. Gunner was Thanatos. He wasn't the murderbot that everybody thought him to be but he did have a body count. Their world was not one of tea, crumpets and forgiveness. Their world was a dangerous and violent one and Gunner had be a part of it long enough to rack up a kill count. She had too.

With nothing else of worth, Mac readied herself to leave. She paused and glanced once more at Aeden's body. She reached over and with a gentle touch of her fingers, closed his eyes. She gently placed a coin over each eye. In every book or movie there was always a soldier who said some shit like *killing never gets any easier* but in truth, it did. It became very easy. She had become numb to it. Killing was a part of her job; it was a part of her life. According to Visegar records, her first kill was on her debut mission she undertook with Gunner.

People applauded her on how well she was handling herself. Nobody applauded the kill, simply how she wasn't breaking down like many agents before her had. The truth was this wasn't her first kill. That kill was one far more memorable.

Bailee reached into the bag of chips and withdrew a small handful. She eagerly put one after another in her mouth as she watched the movie. Holly Silverburgh sat on the couch beside her, eagerly doing the same. It was a Saturday night and the two girls had Gunner's house all to themselves. So the BFFs did what they normally did on a Saturday night, they watched movies. The only difference was without Gunner, they could watch racier movies.

"So where the old man tonight?" Holly asked, her eyes glued to the screen as Matt Dillon parked his jeep.

"He's in Spokane," Bailee lied. "It's some stupid business trip."

The truth was Gunner was in South America on some mission for Operations. He left from time to time for missions such as these but they were growing less frequent. When she was younger she would stay at Holly's house or Rath would *babysit* but lately she had taken to staying on her own.

"Some *business* trip?" Holly said suggestively. "Not spending the weekend with Ms. Hunter?"

"OMG, the Old Man has to stop fucking my teachers," Bailee said with a laugh.

"You should be applauding him. Ms. Hunter is gorgeous," Holly declared. "My dad would *never* let me stay alone for this long while he was on a business trip."

"A) your dad's a plumber. He never has to go on business trips. You get to see him every night."

"My dad *runs* a plumbing business. There is a difference."

"A plumber's crack is a plumber's crack and I've seen

my fair share of your dad's crack." Holly grabbed a cushion and gently smacked her friend with it while declaring her disgust. "And B) the old man told every friend and neighbour to keep an eye on me. I have more eyes on me now than when Gunner's actually here."

The two watched in silence as Denise Richards popped a bottle of champagne. They were watching one of their favourite naughty movies: *Wild Things*. The pair had seen it enough times that they could mouth each word of the script.

"Why do we always watch this film?" Bailee protested.

"We can switch if you want," Holly said with a sinister grin. "We could watch *Into the Blue*."

"No fucking way," Bailee quickly protested. It was spring which meant that it had been almost eight months since her break-up with Millar. Bailee was over him, as much as any girl could be over her first, but being over him didn't mean she wanted to be reminded about him and his ginger Paul Walker looks.

Holly laughed. She shovelled a few more chips into her mouth. The pair watched the TV as the Neve Campbell, Denise Richards and Matt Dillon began to kiss and make out. This was the infamous threesome scene in *Wild Things*. Rumours of this scene were what drew the pair to the movie in the first place, many years ago when they were way too young. Now the scene seemed tame. Yet despite that, Holly seemed to squirm whenever the scene began.

"Did Mr. QB ever try and get you to try this?" Holly asked, "you, him and some cheerleader in some threesome?"

Bailee grabbed the cushion and smacked her friend. "You're an ass."

"Do you miss him?" Holly asked, more seriously this time.

"A little, yeah."

"What about the...." Holly's words trailed off.

"The sex?" Holly nodded. Bailee grabbed the remote

and paused, the screen freezing mid kiss between Neve and Denise. Bailee looked at her friend. Holly had always been hesitant about the topic of sex since the assault from Will Dennehy. Bailee was not much for talking but she was always there for Holly if she needed to open up. If this was her way of opening up and beginning to talk, then Bailee wanted to give her BFF her full attention. "I do miss the sex. It was fun and tender and wild all at once. Now I don't get any and it's been....difficult."

"What is it like when you're with a person like that?"

"It's nice and it's caring," Bailee clumsily explained. She fought to find the right words. She wasn't a wordsmith. She was a high school girl who ran track and secretly trained to be a super soldier. "Robert was kind in that area. It wasn't all about him or all about me. It was about us."

"I want a partner like that," Holly said softly. She grabbed her lip balm and nervously applied it. "They could take me into their arms and hold me but then I could hold them as well."

The two women looked back to the screen. They stared at the two women, forever frozen mid-kiss. Holly looked back at Bailee, a weird expression on her face.

"You're naturally ambidextrous, right?" Holly asked. Bailee nodded. "Did you know that studies say you are twenty-seven percent more likely to be bisexual?"

"Really?" Bailee blinked in surprise. That was a random thought. She glanced back at the screen and stared at the frozen kiss. She looked back at her friend. "Where did you read---?"

Her words were cut off as Holly pressed her lips against Bailee's and the two kissed. For a heartbeat Bailee was simply stunned but eventually she kissed back, curious as to how it would feel. Holly's lips were soft and moist and she tasted of strawberries lip balm. Bailee's lips were firmer and tasted of Sour Cream and Onion chips. The kiss ended and Bailee sat there, stunned.

"Um...hi?" Holly said, unsure what to say next. *Part-*

ner, *they* and *them*, the words ran through Bailee's mind. Holly had been playing the pronoun game. She had avoided saying things like *he, him* and *guy*.

"When did this happen?" Bailee asked, choosing her words carefully. One wrong word and everything could explode.

"I dunno. It kinda evolved that way?" Holly suggested. She nervously bit her lip as she looked for the courage to speak what was in her heart. "Ever since.....that day, whenever I think about being with a guy I get nervous and then anxious and I get scared and I freak out. But when I think about being with a girl, it feels right. I feel safer and I don't feel the same fear and anxiety.

"You're my best friend, Bailee. You have always looked out for me and you were the one to defend me when nobody else could or would. When I think about being with you, I feel protected. I feel safe."

"I love you, Holly. You're my best friend. You are funny and girly and you are always protecting me," Bailee said carefully. "But I don't think I feel that way about girls. I think it's cool that you do. Not that you need it but you have my approval. I will be there for you every step of the way. Nothing changes between us except maybe wording in some of our rules."

"Rules?"

"The rule that once said *we have to approve of each other's boyfriends* will now have to say *we have to approve of each other's boyfriends or girlfriends*." It was joking rule that the girls made in junior high. Holly smiled at the reminder of their old declaration.

"So you're not mad I kissed you?"

"Not at all," Bailee said with a smile. "If somebody had to be your first girl-girl kiss, I'm glad it was me. I'm just sorry that I couldn't be more for you."

"You're already everything I need," Holly said as she wrapped her arms around her BFF. Bailee tried not to wince. Holly was the touchy-feely hugger of the two. Hugging had never been Bailee's thing but she didn't dare break the hug now.

A loud smashing thud at the door split the hug apart as the two girls jumped in shock. Bailee's head snapped around to face the door. Her eyes narrowed as she carefully climbed to her feet. Another smashing knock on the door caused her to jump once more. Before Bailee reached it, the door smashed open. It had been kicked open. Bailee's eyes went wide as she saw Will Dennehy standing in the doorway.

"Will?" she asked cautiously. "What the fuck are you doing here?"

Will stumbled into the house and Bailee backed away. In truth she was putting herself between Will and Holly. Will held a bottle of whiskey in one hand and a baseball bat in the other.

"You fucking ruined my life," Will spat. "You're a fucking cunt who took my future from me."

"Get the fuck out of my house," Bailee snapped. "You're drunk."

"No shit. What else is there to do? I can't play football thanks to you. I can't go to school because without football no school will take me." Will took another swig as he pointed at Bailee with the bat. "I have no football, no job and no school. I have no future because you took it away from me."

"You did that to yourself," Bailee spat. Her eyes moved quickly as she tried to figure out what to do next. From behind her she could hear Holly whimpering in fear. "Just put the bat down."

"The worst part is that ginger pussy is living *my* life. Everybody fucking *loves* Robert Millar." Bailee had followed her ex's career. He was a rising star and everybody knew it. "He's the star and I'm the fucking joke." He lazily swung his bat toward Bailee. The girl quickly shuffled backwards. "It's your fault; it's all your fucking fault."

"Life never turns out how we expect it to," Bailee said, softer this time. If she could get him to lower the bat, then they would be okay. She just had to talk him down. "I lost my parents in a car crash and spent six years, alone, in an orphanage. Life sucks, I know that. But your life isn't over. You can still be happy; you just have to change how you live your life."

Bailee cautiously stepped forward. She slowly reached for the end of the bat and gently pushed it down towards the floor. She spoke softly. "You need to turn around and go home. Sleep this off and I promise things won't be as bad in the morning."

"I...I..." Will let his head drop.

"We all make mistakes," Bailee said. "Yours just cost you a lot more than most."

"I didn't make a mistake!" Suddenly Will was mad again. He swung his booze bottle and smashed it across Bailee's skull. She fell to the ground and Holly screamed. Will snapped his head and his bat towards her, recognizing her for the first time. "You're the lying cunt who started all of this."

Pain assaulted her head as liquid rolled down her face and past her lips. The liquid had a thick coppery taste. Bailee touched the liquid and pulled her hand back. She stared at her red-stained fingers. Blood; she was bleeding from her head. Panic started to fill her mind. She was bleeding from her head. Was she dying?

Holly screamed and Bailee forced herself to focus. She looked over and saw Will drunkenly marching towards her. He was drunkenly yelling and swearing all while menacingly swinging the bat. Bailee pushed herself to her feet. She wouldn't let Will hurt Holly, not now or ever again. Gunner was training her to protect other people. What was the use of these skills if she couldn't protect her best friend?

Bailee stumbled towards Will, her mind quickly racing as she tried to plan her attack. A bat was only useful at the sweet spot. This was a small section of the bat near the end. It was between sixty and seventy-five percent of the bat's length. That was the dangerous area. Anything before or after that sweet spot was pretty much useless in a baseball swing.

"Over here, asshole." Bailee needed his attention

away from Holly. She needed it on her. "Is that all you got, you drunk fuck? Is that the only way you can get hard, by slapping around a couple of girls with a baseball bat?" Bailee was being crass and rude but she needed his attention.

Will turned towards her and readied a swing. Bailee's first reaction was to retreat but Gunner had tried to drill that out of her. A baseball bat was a range weapon. She had to remove that range. Bailee rushed Will and blocked the bat's swing with both arms. She stopped the bat below the sweet spot. The blow still hurt her arms but it was nothing compared to what the sweet spot could have done. Bailee added the arm pain to her ignore list and kept going. She grabbed the bat, twisted and pulled. She tried to pull the bat free but Will wouldn't let go. Her foot lashed out and struck Will's knee, his *right* knee. Fighting a foe she'd already fought meant Bailee already knew where his weaknesses were especially if she was the reason he had them in the first place. Will screamed as his leg buckled. Bailee pulled the bat away and slammed the end into Will's gut. He doubled over in pain before Bailee knocked him to the floor with a second smash. Bailee dropped the bat and kicked it away. She rushed to the couch to see if Holly was alright. Holly leapt from the seat and rushed into Bailee's arms.

"Are you...." Holly froze as she stared at Will. "Behind you!"

Bailee spun around. She saw as Will began to climb back to his feet. Only this time he reached to the back of his belt and pulled free a pistol. Bailee didn't have time to curse or talk him down. Will was already leveling the weapon at her. Bailee just reacted. She grabbed Holly and pulled her to the floor as Bailee dove behind the couch. The first shot rang off and dove into the couch. Holly screamed. Bailee grabbed her friends hand and gave her a stern look.

"When I tell you to go, run for Gunner's study. Do you understand?" Holly nodded quickly. Bailee grabbed the first thing she could find. It happened to be a couch cushion. "Go!"

Holly leapt up and sprinted across the room. Bailee popped up and threw the cushion at Will. It wasn't meant to stop him or slow him. It was meant to be a momentary distraction. When something flew at a person's head, they tried to protect themselves, regardless of what it was. It was human nature. In the brief seconds that Will spent focused on the flying cushion, Bailee bolted after her friend.

Gunner's study was on the main floor of the room. It was a large room with an oak desk, a large TV and a gun rack on the wall. Holly went to the gun rack but Bailee ignored it, she ran to the desk instead. The gun rack was locked and the ammo was in another room. She didn't have time to get both. Instead she pulled open the desk's bottom drawer and gave the inside a punch. A small box fell off the bottom. The box was wrapped in plastic. Bailee tore open the plastic and withdrew the Smith & Wesson M&P pistol that lay within. She grabbed the magazine, slid it into the weapon and drew a fresh round into the chamber.

"What are you doing?" Holly asked.

"I'm ending this," Bailee said as she crouched by a wall.

"Please leave us alone," Holly called out to Will.

"He had his chance," Bailee said. "If he steps into this room, it's over for good."

The two waited in silence as they heard the drunken footsteps of Will. He stumbled towards them, firing a second and third time into a wall or a random piece of furniture. He called their names out, loud and menacingly. Each syllable was a promise of the punishment that each deserved for wronging him. They were to blame for his life. They were the bringers of his destruction. Bailee's mind was set. If their survival was only achieved by death, then she would kill Will. Yet her mind hesitated. She didn't want to kill. There was no coming back after taking a life. Gunner always said that it changed a person. Bailee hoped Will turned around and walked away, she prayed for it. She hoped he'd drop the gun or he'd trip and fall and pass out. She wasn't ready to change.

Will stumbled into the study. He spotted Holly across the room and once again leveled his pistol at her. Any hesitation that resided in Bailee instantly vanished as Gunner's training kicked in. Bailee rose from her crouch. The M&P fired twice, putting a round in Will's leg and gut. Bailee leveled the weapon at Will's head and squeezed off a third round. The 9mm round tore through his skull and brought everything to an end. The body fell to the ground. It didn't fade away or vanish; it just lay on the floor as blood began to slowly pool. "Is...is he..." Holly's word trailed off. Bailee lowered her weapon and nodded. She walked to the desk and grabbed Gunner's landline phone. She punched in the emergency number he'd made her memorize years ago.

"Go for Ops."

"Emergency Code: Romeo-478-Whiskey-Mario."

"Connecting."

Bailee waited in silence for several moments until a familiar voice suddenly spoke.

"Bailee, its Rath. What's wrong?"

"Someone just broke into our house. He attacked us and I...he's dead now."

"Shit. Are you okay?"

"I'm bleeding from the head," Bailee answered. For the first time since she's pulled the trigger, the pain suddenly returned. Her arms ached, her head was throbbing and the room was growing increasingly dizzy. "Fuck, I'm hurt, Rath."

"Call the cops."

"I can't. I used a clean gun, I have a witness and I have history with the guy."

"How bad?"

"It's the sheriff's boy."

"The one from last year?"

"Yeah."

"Is the witness a threat?" Bailee looked at Holly. Her friend was standing over Will's body, motionless. She stared down at the corpse. Then suddenly she spat on his and kicked the body twice.

"She's good."

"I'll have a team there in fifteen minutes. I'll be there myself in an hour and I'm recalling Gunner. You just need to make sure you're okay." Rath ordered. "Will you be okay? If not, call the cops. We'll deal with the fallout. Did you copy?"

Bailee looked at the gun in her hand. It felt heavy and cold. It felt foreign. Bailee looked around the study. Everything seemed duller. The study was normally a wonderful room that radiated life and strength. Now it just seemed monotonous, like colour had faded or overcast had taken hold of the sky.

"Bailee? Bailee?" Rath yelled into the phone. "God damn it, Bailee, answer me."

"It's Mac," she eventually replied, a stern tone taking hold of her voice. "Call me Mac."

CHAPTER 10

"Raven this is *Trautman* Actual."

"Go for Raven."

"We've got some more intel on these new Death Hounds," Keane said. "We've identified all five members."

"Four," Bailee corrected.

"The four *remaining* are Morozko, Dryad, Ultraviolet and Renata Shatalov," Keane explained.

"Morozko is ice user," Mac said. "I think I just saw the speedster Ultraviolet and I met Renata Shatalov."

"Dryad is Einin Moran. She can control nature. We don't have much on her power levels."

"Tell me about Shatalov."

"This took a while to find. Shatalov wasn't her original name," Ford explained. "She was born under another name." He paused for a moment. "Is this intel important to the mission?"

"Yes," Mac said. She was growing tired of Ford's reluctant to give information. Why was he holding back? "Spill it."

"She was born Reneta Lentsov," Ford explained. "Her father was Sergey Lentsov. He was a member of the original Death Hounds. He was killed by Thanatos. When they began cleaning the unit, Sergey's wife, Zara Shatalov, fled to France with her daughter. She ditched her married name and returned to her maiden one.

didn't know it at the time but she saved him.

"There," Mac said as she pointed to the screen. "That's the third time that van had passed the building. They know we're here." Mac turned around and yelled to Gunner. "Hurry up, Old Man. We're about to get company."

"We just got the call," a new voice said. A large man - Lt. Ashley Latif - stepped into the room. He stopped before Shatalov and saluted. "The intruder is heading to the armoury."

"Send two platoons," Shatalov ordered. "We know what she's capable of and we know what she can do. We are going to ambush her and this time we will be successful."

"Dead or alive, Ma'am?"

"Kill her," the Major ordered. "Kill Mac."

Their boots made a roaring thunder as thirty pairs stormed the armoury. Lt. Brooks led the team and ordered each soldier to spread out. One by one, the soldiers moves, covering each entrance and exit and hiding amongst the shadows. When Mac came in, she would be surrounded. They wouldn't wait to fire or engage in banter, they would simply gun her down.

But Mac never showed.

Mac saw each of the Whitestar soldiers frantically move as they took position. She watched it all on the security feed. Mac sat the main desk in the security building and watched the various feed from across the base. Two Whitestar goons lay scattered about the floor beside her, unconscious. Mac leaned back in her chair and frowned. This attempted ambush was the proof she was looking for. She had a leak.

The question now was whether the leak was from someone intercepting her radio transmissions or from someone on her team? After the vehicle bay she suspected a leak but she still needed proof. This was why she said she was going to the armoury when she was really heading to the security offices. Now she had her proof.

Mac pushed back on her wheeled chair and rolled across the room. She stopped at a mini-fridge and opened it up. She looked at the pop and dismissed it. Caffeine was a powerful tool but she also didn't want a sugar crash. She grabbed a bottle of water and twisted off the lid. She also grabbed an apple and with a smile, rolled back to the screens. The fingers of one hand eagerly tapped the keys as her other hand lifted the apple to her mouth. Mac hungrily fed on the fruit, savouring the sweet taste. Eating an apple on a mission, Gunner would be proud.

She cycled through the cameras in the dorms and paused as she reached the kitchen. There, seated in the center of the room, were the hostages. Each was zip tied and seated on the floor. She moved through the gaggle of hostages and looked for familiar faces. She didn't seen Rath's mask or Gunner's face but she did see DJ. She needed to talk to him.

"DJ, can you hear me?" Mac said aloud. He watched the screen as DJ's head shot up. His eyes narrowed as he focused.

Erik 'DJ' Ruckas was a skinny blonde sniper. His meta ability was enhanced hearing. His ability kicked in at puberty and his hearing amplified. His teenage brain was literally assaulted by every noise imaginable. From the scraping of a pencil, to the clicking of nails, the flapping of insect wings and the whispers of a young boy two blocks away, DJ heard it all. Normally music was his release. He could hide behind the music but without it he needed a great deal of concentration to drown out the world.

"I'm at your 1:30." DJ turned his head slightly to the right and scanned the wall until he found the camera. He gave the camera a small nod. "Are you okay?" DJ nodded again.

tages in this room, each bound like he was. There was Agent: Blindspot, two of his assistants, two scientists and Morrell Blood's Head of Operations, Orlando Trumbo. They were held in a small room deep within the laboratory building. The rest of the hostages were in the dorms. There were five guards surrounding them. It didn't take Gunner long to deduce that they were Whitestar.

He *hated* Whitestar.

There were also two metas who walked in and out of the room. One was a tall Russian and the other was an African-American woman with purple hair. If they had two metas here, then they had more in the field. That left WhiteStar's senior staff. Major Renata Shatalov had come in and out of the hostage room. She'd make a speech, threaten Agent: Blindspot and then vanish. She was the boss of the Death Hounds and everybody knew it.

An unlocking sound filled the room and Gunner turned his attention to the opening doors. Shatalov entered the room. Gunner eyed the woman. She was older than most of the soldiers in the base. Her face looked worn and tired. Yet, despite her age, her body was firm and in good shape. She wore a black tactical vest over a dark turtleneck sweater. On her hip was a Glock 17. Hanging from a sling around her neck was a FN P90. Gunner knew she was French Special Forces, he'd seen enough of them to pick her out by her weapon loadout, but there was still so much he didn't know about her.

Shatalov stepped aside as two goons dragged a familiar body into the room. They dumped an unconscious Rath on the floor and laughed. Shatalov gave the body a kick and Rath let out a groan. The men shoved him against the wall.

"Unlock the project," Shatalov calmly ordered. "Or more will end up like him."

"You'll never get my codes," Blindspot spat. "You can hurt us all you want."

"I dislike causing unnecessary harm," Shatalov explained. "Ms. Kaluuya, however, enjoys inflicting pain. She enjoys knifes and knows how to use them."

"I'm not telling you the codes."

"I will get them, one way or another, however the longer I take, the more people Ms. Kaluuya will hurt."

"Boss, we have Dryad incoming." Shatalov turned to her second in command, Lieutenant Ashley Latif. She gave him a nod. The soldier left the room only to return, seconds later, with Dryad.

"What do you want?" Shatalov asked.

"My brother," Einin said, her words were broken and pain filled. "Aeden is dead. That bitch killed her."

Shatalov turned to face her. Dryad's face was stained with dried tears. Shatalov reached out and placed her hand on the Irish woman's shoulder. "I'm sorry, Einin. Your brother didn't deserve to die here."

"She shot him," she explained as tears choked her words. "She shot him point blank, in the head."

"Who is this girl?"

"She said her name was Mac."

Gunner's eyed narrowed. He tried to hear what they were saying. Mac? Mac was here? Of course she was here. A hostage situation like this was normally handled by him. Gunner was Ops' go-to man but if he was out of commission who would they turn to next? They'd turn to his girl; they'd turn to Mac. He'd trained her for exactly that purpose.

Rath let out a roar as he smashed open a set of steel doors. The metal had no chance against Rath's strength; it simply bent, buckled and broke. Gunner entered the room, his hands firmly grasping the Glock 17. Gunner moved into the building first as Mac and Rath followed. Rath held SIG Sauer P226 - although he rarely used it - while Mac carried a FN P90 as she pulled up the rear. The trio moved quickly as a unit, breaching and clearing room after room. They were moving through the safe house for a meta group known as

MetaNow. They were a terrorist movement set on breaking the meta-truth to the world through act of violence and exposure. Gunner was here to stop them.

Gunner had spent three weeks tearing through cell after cell of the organization. They were scattered and uncoordinated. Gunner had often wondered what threat they could have been if they had real leadership.

They breached the final room. It was filled to the brim with servers and computers, each humming as it produced data. Rath cursed as he saw their find. "It'll take tech a week to decode this."

"We don't have a week," Gunner said. He plopped down at what looked to be the main computer and quickly started tapping on the keys. "We need to know the location and now."

Chatter had spoken of a MetaNow terrorist attack set to go off in two days. Gunner wasn't going to let that happen. His fingers got to work as he quickly typed. Rath glanced at Mac. She was standing by the security camera. Her fingers were also busy, flipping through each channel as she searched the streets below.

"Hey, Bailee," Rath began.

"It's Mac," she corrected.

"How you doing?" This wasn't Mac's first mission, it was only her third, but Rath still saw the shiver in her hand as she held a gun.

"I'm good, big guy," Mac replied. She kept flipping through the channels. "The Old Man promised to bring me to Paris one day." Mac pointed to the nearest window. Rath looked out the window and over the Paris cityscape. "I just never thought it'd be on a mission."

"It's never good enough for kids these days," Rath joked.

"I *am* an entitled girl," Mac joked.

Gunner stole a glance at the two. For a moment his fingers paused their typing. It was surreal seeing Mac on a mission. He knew this was the outcome of her training but now he doubted his decision. He didn't want to lose her. He wasn't ashamed to say that. He liked the girl, she was special to him. Mac wasn't Clara, no woman was. Gunner tried to shake the memory of his wife away but it clung tightly. Soon it was joined by the memories of Laura and Sondra. Each was a woman he'd lost. Each was a woman who died. He wouldn't let Mac be next.

It was his lifestyle that cost the life of Clara, his wife. She was killed by Hector Symone, a hired sniper whose shot went wide. It was bullet meant for Gunner that ended up in Clara's lung. Gunner was devastated when she died. First he found rage, than he found Hector and then he found an empty spot in his heart, the spot vengeance had failed to heal. He tried everything to fill it. That led to Laura.

Laura was a NYPD cop. She was an honest cop and a good one. She was working on vice cases when she met Gunner. The two were good for each other and more importantly, they had fun together. Laura died when a sting went bad. She was gunned down by some gang-banger named Tido. Gunner found rage and then he found Tido. He didn't kill the banger, Laura wouldn't have wanted that, but he did make sure the man never walked again. Empty once more, Gunner sought to fill his heart. This led to Sondra.

Sondra was an operative, just like him. She worked for Visegar and she was good. She was a tech wiz and could read a person a mile away. She was assigned to Gunner on several missions and the two become close. It started out as just nasty, kinky sex that passed the endless hours stuck in a safe house and then feelings got in the way. She died trying to defuse a bomb. She didn't succeed but she delayed the detonation long enough for Gunner to escape. Empty once more, Gunner was ready to swear off people. He was ready to accept the hermit life. Then he found Mac.

Now, as he stared at her and Rath, he wondered if he had made the right choice. He hesitated even adopting her, worrying what it would be like to put himself out there again, but looking back, it was the smartest decision of his life. She didn't know it at the time but she saved him.

"There," Mac said as she pointed to the screen. "That's the third time that van had passed the building. They know we're here." Mac turned around and yelled to Gunner. "Hurry up, Old Man. We're about to get company."

"We just got the call," a new voice said. A large man - Lt. Ashley Latif - stepped into the room. He stopped before Shatalov and saluted. "The intruder is heading to the armoury."

"Send two platoons," Shatalov ordered. "We know what she's capable of and we know what she can do. We are going to ambush her and this time we will be successful."

"Dead or alive, Ma'am?"

"Kill her," the Major ordered. "Kill Mac."

Their boots made a roaring thunder as thirty pairs stormed the armoury. Lt. Brooks led the team and ordered each soldier to spread out. One by one, the soldiers moves, covering each entrance and exit and hiding amongst the shadows. When Mac came in, she would be surrounded. They wouldn't wait to fire or engage in banter, they would simply gun her down.

But Mac never showed.

Mac saw each of the Whitestar soldiers frantically move as they took position. She watched it all on the security feed. Mac sat the main desk in the security building and watched the various feed from across the base. Two Whitestar goons lay scattered about the floor beside her, unconscious. Mac leaned back in her chair and frowned. This attempted ambush was the proof she was looking for. She had a leak.

The question now was whether the leak was from someone intercepting her radio transmissions or from someone on her team? After the vehicle bay she suspected a leak but she still needed proof. This was why she said she was going to the armoury when she was really heading to the security offices. Now she had her proof.

Mac pushed back on her wheeled chair and rolled across the room. She stopped at a mini-fridge and opened it up. She looked at the pop and dismissed it. Caffeine was a powerful tool but she also didn't want a sugar crash. She grabbed a bottle of water and twisted off the lid. She also grabbed an apple and with a smile, rolled back to the screens. The fingers of one hand eagerly tapped the keys as her other hand lifted the apple to her mouth. Mac hungrily fed on the fruit, savouring the sweet taste. Eating an apple on a mission, Gunner would be proud.

She cycled through the cameras in the dorms and paused as she reached the kitchen. There, seated in the center of the room, were the hostages. Each was zip tied and seated on the floor. She moved through the gaggle of hostages and looked for familiar faces. She didn't seen Rath's mask or Gunner's face but she did see DJ. She needed to talk to him.

"DJ, can you hear me?" Mac said aloud. He watched the screen as DJ's head shot up. His eyes narrowed as he focused.

Erik 'DJ' Ruckas was a skinny blonde sniper. His meta ability was enhanced hearing. His ability kicked in at puberty and his hearing amplified. His teenage brain was literally assaulted by every noise imaginable. From the scraping of a pencil, to the clicking of nails, the flapping of insect wings and the whispers of a young boy two blocks away, DJ heard it all. Normally music was his release. He could hide behind the music but without it he needed a great deal of concentration to drown out the world.

"I'm at your 1:30." DJ turned his head slightly to the right and scanned the wall until he found the camera. He gave the camera a small nod. "Are you okay?" DJ nodded again.

"Tap code time: Where is Gunner?" DJ elevated his bound hands slightly, not enough to catch the guards' attention but enough for the camera to clearly see, and started tapping his thumbs.

Tap code was a code system that involved a five-by-five grid. Each square had a letter and by tapping two numbers, DJ could spell out a word, one letter at a time. Mac watched as DJ first tapped his right thumb against his fist and then tapped his left. One right and three left meant L. Mac grabbed a pencil and paper and started writing down what he tapped.

3,1 - L
1,1 - A
1,2 - B

"Is Agent: Blindspot with him?" DJ nodded. "And Rath?" DJ shrugged. It made sense. He would have seen Rath being dragged out but couldn't have known where he was being dragged to. DJ probably had a good idea with his hearing but couldn't know for sure.

"Any meta's with you?" DJ started tapping once more.

2,4 - I
1,3 - C
1,5 - E
1,2 - B
3,1 - L
1,1 - A
4,3 - S
4,4 - T
1,5 - E
4,2 - R

Ice blaster, he meant Morozko. Mac scanned the room once again but didn't see the tall Russian.

"He comes and goes?" DJ nodded.

"Does he use any schedule?" DJ shook his head.

"Are you armed?" DJ shook his head.

"I'm coming for you, DJ," Mac promised. "Be ready to move on my command." DJ nodded.

Mac typed on the keyboard and cycled through the laboratory feeds but she found several out. She paused on one room and stared at the familiar face of Gunner. She frowned. The man was seated next to a garnet haired woman - one of the scientists - flirting with her. In truth he was keeping her calm but Mac had seen this move enough times to know. She rolled her eyes. Only Gunner could find himself a hostage and wind up with a date. She was at least relieved to see that the Old Man was okay. Rath was another story. He was cut and beaten. From what Mac could see from the feed, he had been cut with a set of knives by someone with a skilled and practised hand.

"*Trautman*, come in."

"Go for *Trautman*." Ford's voice came over the radio. "Are any of the Death Hounds an interrogation specialist?" Mac regretted what the answer would be.

"Checking."

Mac knelt by the first unconscious soldier and began to search his gear. After knocking each of them out, the first thing she did was remove each of their weapons. Now, with more time on her hands, she started to look and see if they had anything useful on them. She started with the M4 ammo and pocketed that. Next she took a look at grenades. Each of them had two frags, she pocketed them, but what really caught her attention were the two flash bangs grenades.

Flash bang grenades - also known as stun grenades or sound bombs - were a non-lethal explosive device used to temporarily disorient an enemy's senses. When detonated it produces a blinding light and an intensely loud bang. Mac smiled. She had an idea brewing. She searched every cabinet until she found a spool of wire, a roll of duct tape and several sets of disposable earplugs. Mac's smile grew wider.

"I've got what you want, Raven," Ford said suddenly.

"Go ahead."

"Ultraviolet is a trained interrogation specialist," Ford started. Mac sighed. It had to be the speedster. "Ops have used her to extract intel. She has a decent record and a highly skilled hand for it."

"Highly skill hand but only a decent record?" Mac asked.

"Kaluuya tends to go too far. She seems to draw pleasure from a kill."

"This is just fucking great," Mac muttered. "What horrible fucking back-story makes a speedster with a murder spree?"

"Kaluuya grew up with two middle-class parents. They were a church going family from some mining town in Nowhere, USA. They were a picture perfect family. Father was a miner and coached little league while Mother was a pharmacist's assistant while working on the PTA." Mac listened intently as she waited for the foot to drop because with metas, it *always* dropped. "When the mine closed, Kaluuya's father had trouble finding work. He became a bit of drunk and started to get angry and eventually turned violent. He started to strike his wife. Eventually the wife fought back. She stabbed and killed her husband. She was arrested and is serving a life sentence. Phylicia and her younger brother Theo were put into foster care. They bounced from home to home until they were eventually separated. When Phylicia turned sixteen she became an emancipated minor and moved out on her own.

"The company found her when she was seventeen years. She was working two jobs trying to make enough money to look after herself and Theo. The company offered her a job with the promise of a big salary and the guarantee that Theo would always be looked after. Phylicia willingly allowed Visegar to experiment on her. They recreated her trauma in order to activate her Lycotta gene. She developed super-speed. With her new powers she asked to be an operative.

"She did numerous missions with us, both at home

and away, and proved to be an invaluable asset. She trained with some of our torture experts so she could be an interrogator. It wasn't until several red flags showed up - people dying when they shouldn't have or her performing actions that were highly dangerous - that she was reevaluated and eventually benched."

"What did the psychological evaluations reveal?" Mac asked.

"Phylicia Kaluuya was diagnosed with borderline personality disorder and post traumatic stress disorder," Ford answered. "Her mother didn't kill her father, she did. Her mother simply took the blame. She needed help and we were more than happy to offer it to her but Kaluuya didn't want it. Whitestar came a knocking and she quickly jumped ship."

"Fuck," Mac said. "She's been torturing Rath and I don't know why. What the hell are they looking for?"

"I don't know, Raven," Grammer Ford said. "Everything I find is way above my pay grade."

"Thanks. Raven: out."

Mac moved for the door but paused. She glanced at the weapon rack by the door and spotted a black forward handgrip lying on the shelf. Mac grabbed it and quickly attached it to her M4. Mac preferred the forward handgrip on a rifle. It allowed her a steadier aim and granted her the ability to pull the weapon tighter into her shoulder. Mac tested her grip on the forward with her left hand and smirked. Now she was ready to free DJ.

CHAPTER 11

Mac pulled open the side door and crept into the dorms. Years of training from Gunner had taught her how to move swiftly without sacrificing her stealth. Her rifle was held firm in both hands, moving with her eyes as she scanned each hallway and paused at each door. The dorms had dozens of rooms, which meant there were dozens of places for WhiteStar goons to hide. Clearing a building would be done with a team no smaller than four. A building as large as the dorms would require several teams of four to safely secure but Mac didn't have several teams, she didn't even have a team of four. There was only her. She was the lone intruder in a base full of soldiers. She felt like a damn Hollywood cliché.

Mac spotted a lone female soldier patrolling the hallways. She ducked into a dorm room and waited for the woman to pass. She emerged behind her and struck quickly. Her foot lashed out and caught the back of the soldier's knee. Her leg buckled as he tried to turn around. Her face looked back just in time to see the butt of Mac's rifle coming at her. Mac smashed the butt of her rifle across the soldier's face and sent her spinning to the ground. She dropped onto the solider's body, pressing her knee into the woman's neck. Mac snapped up her rifle and aimed down the hallway. Mac needed to keep an eye out in case others approached. She pressed with her knee until the body beneath her stopped moving. She eased off the unconscious woman's neck. She grabbed the soldier by the vest and pulled her into the side room. Mac worked quickly. First she robbed the woman of her ammo and grenades. Then she stole her knife. Mac took her stolen SIG Sauer P226 and pressed the knife against its barrel. Then she quickly taped them together, creating a makeshift bayonet for the pistol. Mac had a six point plan to freeing DJ. Point one was complete. She needed to prepare point two.

Mac checked the last pockets and found a pair of black sunglasses. Mac smirked as she relieved the woman of them. Mac slid them onto her own face and glanced into the mirror to check out her reflection. They were a pair of Oakley Conductor sunglasses but more importantly, they looked damn good on her.

DJ was bored, he was *very* bored. All day he had done little but sit on his ass. It was an activity he enjoyed at home but at least there he wasn't a hostage. He glanced at the eight WhiteStar goons. They were as bored as he was. They didn't want to be here but this was easy money for them. Or it was until Mac showed up. DJ smiled at the thought. Mac was here to save them and she was going to kick their fucking asses.

Mac was a thing of legends. When they first met, DJ was already working for Ops. He thought she was some rookie that he'd have to train but it was completely the opposite. She was assembling a team - her team - and she wanted him on it. She broke down the design and he was sold. Mac helped perfect his training. He was unbeatable with the long gun but shit with the short. She taught him how to shoot small arms and how to fight. Her reasoning was that not all of their missions would allow for a sniper and his powers were too important to be left out.

"DJ," Mac's voice suddenly filled his ear. She was elsewhere, speaking in a low tone but to him it was as if she was speaking directly into his ear. He looked up at the camera.

"There is no way for you to respond so listen.

"I'm outside the kitchen. I will breach the room and strike. I'm using flash bangs; protect yourself. Get free and start shooting. We're going to clear this room quickly."

DJ blinked in confusion. How was he going to free himself from these zip ties? How was he going to shoot without a gun? Wait, did she say flash bangs?

"Breach in -- 5," Mac said. DJ tilted his head to the left and pressed his left ear against his left shoulder. He awkwardly pressed the back of his left hand against his right ear.

4

DJ closed his eyes and kept them tightly shut. He took a deep breath and tried to focus. A flash bang was meant to be loud. It would make a noise greater than 170 decibels. Loud noises hurt most people; it would be hell for him.

3

DJ had to protect himself. He had to focus his super hearing away from the room and onto something else. Much like how a normal person could eventually tune out the sound of a noisy fridge or creaking pipes, he could tune out all the sounds in a room. It was difficult but not impossible.

2

DJ focuses on the sound of his heart. Beat after beat, in a steady tone, echoed in his ears. It was a hypnotic sound that, if done correctly, could be the only sound DJ heard.

1

Thump, thump, thump and thump. One after another the beats grew louder and louder until there was nothing else except the thumps. There was no laughter, no chatter or no fearful sobs. There was only thump after thump.

Breach

The mess door opened slightly as two flash bangs bounced into the room. The WhiteStar soldiers spun around just in time to see them explode. A lucky few covered their eyes or dove for cover but most screamed in pain as the blinding light filled the room and assaulted their eyes. Mac kicked open the door, her eyes covered by the Oakley shades, and slid the stolen SIG Sauer across the floor. She then gripped her rifle with both hand, brought it upwards and opened fire.

DJ felt something bump into his foot. He opened his eyes, snapped out of his trance and stared down at the gun that lay before him. It was a SIG Sauer P226 WhiteStar Tactical with a knife taped to it. DJ dropped his hands and used the blade to cut the plastic ties. DJ grabbed the gun, pulled off the knife and pointed it at the nearest WhiteStar goon. His pistol snapped to life as he put two bullets into the goon's body. DJ kept to his knees as he scanned the room. He ignored the goons affected by the bang and instead looked for the one smart enough to cover their eyes and ears. He spotted the WhiteStar muscle head in the distance with shades on his face. The man had been wearing sunglasses all day and not once had he stepped outdoors. He was the type of douche that wore sunglasses at night like he was Corey Hart. DJ leveled his weapon at Capt. Shades and smirked.

"The eighties are over," DJ mumbled to himself before pulling the trigger twice. Capt. Shades dropped. DJ felt proud of his two KOs and was hoping for a third yet as he looked around the room he found the remaining six had been bested.

Mac was the thing of legends.

"Clear," Mac said loudly.

"Clear," DJ replied.

Mac moved to the mess door and quickly reloaded her weapons. DJ scrambled to the nearest fallen goon and acquired himself a stolen rifle. He grabbed an undamaged tactical vest and pulled it over his shoulders. He squirmed as he adjusted the straps to make it fit. His tall, lean form always made for difficulty in getting most gear to fit.

"Holy shit," a female voice said suddenly. "You're her; you're Mac."

Murmurs filled the room. Mac turned around and stared at the woman. She was a middle-eastern woman with penny-coloured hair and deep eyes. She was clearly a soldier. The woman snapped to attention and gave Mac a salute. Mac rolled her eyes.

"I'm Lt. Rivka Eizenkot," the woman introduced. "I was assigned here as military support."

"You're the girl from the Israel Defense Force, aren't you?" Eizenkot nodded. Mac had heard about her. She was a powerless soldier but she was a damn good one. She first reached Mac's ears when word that the company had gotten a recruit from the IDF was going around. IDF acquisitions were rare, even more so with women. IDF soldiers were bad asses but they were also loyal to a fault. Sounds of yelling could be heard from outdoors. Mac pointed to the dead bodies on the floor. "Get your men on their feet. Everybody grab a weapon and some ammunition and take position. WhiteStar will be punching through here any minute now and I have a six point plan on how to defeat them."

"A six point plan?" DJ asked.

"Point one was to acquire you a gun and a knife," Mac explained.

"Point two was to rescue me?"

The sound of a detonating grenade echoed from down the hall. Mac looked back at DJ. "Point two was to booby trap the entrances with grenades. It'll slow them down."

"Was point three coming to save me?" Mac glared at DJ. He shrugged. "I'll stop asking."

Eizenkot smirked at Mac. She was beginning to like the woman. Lt. Eizenkot turned around and ordered her troops to their feet. One by one she handed out any weapon she could find. She gave a rifle to one and a pistol to another. Then she placed them around the mess hall behind overturned tables and chairs. She ordered the non-combatives to the farthest point from the doors. Eizenkot moved without hesitation or fear. She had to prove that she was worthy of this job, especially in front of the legendary Mac. She had heard rumours about that woman. Mac was strong as an ox. Mac was faster than a cheetah. Mac was unstoppable. Mac was the super soldier. She didn't know which ones she believed and which she didn't - Eizenkot had been in the military long enough to know not to believe everything - but she did know that she wanted to impress the woman.

"Incoming: six on us in twelve seconds." DJ called out the numbers as he heard them.

"Ready!" Eizenkot yelled as she raised her own rifle. She stared down the reflex sight and aimed it at the open doors. Eizenkot steadied her breathing as she waited for the first form to pass before her. A second later a large man stepped in the doorway and Eizenkot opened fire. She put a pair of 5.56×45mm NATO rounds into the man and watched him fall to the floor.

The room became a fire fight. WhiteStar troops poured into the room from both ends and guns on either side of the conflict roared to life. DJ fired and moved. Eizenkot marveled how the sniper could bob and weave, moving at the last second to avoid enemy fire. She'd heard how his hearing was so good that he could hear a bullet approach and move with enough time to avoid being shot. It was an impressive skill. It didn't hurt that DJ was fairly good looking as well.

Mac was a machine. She fought like a woman possessed. Her rifle roared to life and her body never stopped moving. When she wasn't shooting, she was fighting. She'd kick out an enemy's limb, strike down an opponent or simply jab at them with her rifle barrel before tossing them to the floor like discarded trash. Eizenkot knew she was a damn good soldier, Mac was just better.

Eizenkot backed away from the door. Her M4 snapped off round after round. She fired with exceptional accuracy. She killed those unfortunate enough to find themselves before her sights and suppressed those smart enough to stay behind cover. Eizenkot glanced over her shoulder and saw a WhiteStar goon sneaking up on Mac. He had a shotgun in his hand and was leveling it at her back. Eizenkot didn't think; she just reacted. She pivoted around and bolted at the man. She leapt over a chair and slid across a counter, her rifle firing as she skimmed the countertop. The burst of three riddled his chest and sent him flying backwards. He fell over and fired into the roof. Mac spun around only to see Eizenkot standing over the fallen body. Mac looked at the woman and gave her a nod before pivoting back to battle. Eizenkot found her inner self cheering loudly. She'd just gotten a nod of approval from the Mac.

"They're pulling back," DJ said with a tilt of his head.

"Did we win?" one of the soldiers asked. Mac ignored them all. She quickly reloaded her weapon. Mac glanced at Eizenkot and nodded to the fallen corpses of both WhiteStar and Visegar. Eizenkot nodded back.

"Reload your guns. Then loot the bodies for ammo and gear. If you have a pistol, grab a riffle," Eizenkot barked. "If you have nothing, get your hands on a goddamn gun, now."

More unarmed Visegar soldiers emerged from their cover and started grabbing weapons and vest. They filled their pockets with ammunition. Mac moved to the door and peered outside. She'd heard three detonations during the battle. This meant three of her four booby trapped doors had gone off. She glanced down the hallway and spotted two goons approaching. Two rounds later and they were instead lying on the floor, dead.

"Incoming!" Mac turned to DJ and saw a look of fear on his face.

"How many?" Eizenkot asked.

"Just one." Five second later Mac heard the noise that DJ feared so much. It was a hum, moving through the base. The speedster was approaching.

"Take cover."

A violet blur, accompanied by a loud hum, ripped through the mess hall. In the blink of an eye three Visegar soldiers fell to the floor, their throats cut open. The hum came to a halt as the violet blur came to a halt and shimmered into view. Standing before them was Ultraviolet, the psychopathic speedster.

"There is nothing as intoxicating as watching the last breath of life escape the lungs," her voice was still and calm. If she was excited, it didn't show in her voice. "I cherish that moment but rarely do I get to savour it in battle."

Mac, DJ and Eizenkot each raised their rifles and aimed it at Ultraviolet. She looked at the three and smiled. It wasn't a real smile, it was a fake one. It was the smile a person gave when they felt they *had* to smile instead of *wanting* to smile. It was a creepy fake smile.

"Too often I am forced to rush a kill, to speed up that final breath. I simply want to slow down and savour my work." She held her knives up to show. They were long curved blades. They were jagged so to tear flesh with greater ease, they were simple blades sharpened like a scalpel. "These are my tools. They are what I use in my craft. These will be the instruments of your death."

DJ fired first. A burst of three rounds ripped through the air. In the blink of an eye, Ultraviolet dodged each. DJ fired again only this time Eizenkot joined him. Two three-round burst came at her, from two different directions, but neither hit Ultraviolet. A hum filled the air as she dodged four rounds and, just to show off, deflected the remaining two with her knives. Ultraviolet dashed at Mac and slammed her open palm into Mac's chest. Mac flew backward and smashed into a wall. She winced; she could feel the pain in her chest. If Mac was lucky then she'd just bruised a rib. She eyed Ultraviolet and saw a sinister smile staring back. The speedster could have killed her there but she didn't. She was showing off.

"I was instructed only to kill you, Mac, but if your friends persist in shooting at me, then I'll be forced to kill everybody here." Mac winced as she waved their weapons down. DJ and Eizenkot reluctantly placed their weapons the floor. Mac let hers hang from the sling. She slowly let her hand drop to her belt. Ultraviolet smirked. "Good girl. See how things get when people obey me."

"Fuck you," DJ spat. Ultraviolet became a momentary blur. When she returned to focus she had DJ by the neck and had slammed him against the wall, several feet in the air. DJ gasped for air.

"Say that again," she taunted. "Draw one final breath

and say that again."

Ultraviolet watched in with carnal yearning as DJ tried to draw a breath. She watched in ecstasy as he failed. Her grip was too strong for his lungs to draw oxygen. He was going to die in her hands.

A spinning kick slammed into her side. The blow snapped the speedster from her reverie. She turned her head only to see Eizenkot's fist slam against her face. Ultraviolet released DJ as she fell to the floor. DJ slid down the wall and slammed against the mess floor with a sickening thud. Time slowed as Ultraviolet called upon her speed. She glanced at Eizenkot. The woman was reaching for the pistol on her waist. She slowly drew it and leveled it her. Ultraviolet cursed. How? How had this soldier been able to creep on her? She knew the answer. She had been focused on her kill. Once again she had been focused on her obsession. No more.

Rage filled Ultraviolet. She drew both her blade and dashed towards the soldier. To everybody else it all occurred in a blur but to the speedster it was a carefully planned attack. She thrust both blades into Eizenkot's chest. Using the speed and momentum, she hoisted Eizenkot's body into the air and then she slowed. She came into focus and everybody in the mess gasped as they saw Eizenkot, hoisted in the air by Ultraviolet, with a pair of knives run through her. Ultraviolet stood there for a moment and let the horror of the situation fill each and every one of their eyes. She would haunt their memories and she would be the fear they felt until the last pitiful moments of their life.

"They all die," Ultraviolet said as she tossed the corpse of Eizenkot to the floor. It bounced off of the floor and slid until it came to a halt. Ultraviolet panted as rage poured out of each of her pores. "I will kill everybody here and you will be forced to watch. I will mutilate them all while you stand by, unable to do anything. I will ---"

Her screams fell to a halt as she heard the metallic ting of a bouncing canister. She looked at the floor and saw a flash bang bouncing towards her. Mac had pulled the grenade and primed it, waiting until the very last second before tossing it. Ultraviolet called on her speed and dove behind a table, closing her eyes and covering her ears as she did.

"You fucking bitch!" Kaluuya yelled. She popped up from behind her cover only to find Mac gone. "You think you can run from me?"

Ultraviolet called on her speed and sped after the escaping soldier. She tore down one hallway and turned the corner into another. The speedster spotted Mac at the end of the hallway, crouched with her M4 aimed directly at her. Mac squeezed the trigger and fired on full automatic mode. The M4 assault rifle had the ability to shoot between 700-950 rounds per minute. So in the single second that Mac spent firing at the speedster, she had send fifteen rounds down the hallway. Ultraviolet pivoted on her feet and pitched herself into the nearest room. She crashed into the floor, inertia being the bitch it was, and Ultraviolet cursed the pain. She was really starting to hate Mac.

"You think that's going to stop me?" she yelled at the soldier. "I will rip your throat open and watch you die. I'll use my speed and slow down time. I'll spend what seems like hours watching you fucking die."

Mac didn't respond. Ultraviolet stuck her head out of the room and glanced down the hallway. Mac was nowhere to be seen. In the distance she could hear the footsteps of her fleeing. Did this Mac think she could outrun her? Did she think she could outrun Phylicia Kaluuya, the speedster? She scoffed at the idea. Ultraviolet exited the room and took off running. Originally Ultraviolet had no desire to kill Mac. She was ordered to kill the woman and she would enjoy the kill, but Ultraviolet had no beef with the woman. Now, things had changed. At the moment she wanted nothing more in this world then to kill the soldier. She wanted to rip Mac open piece by piece and savour the euphoria that came with a kill. Now, she felt an unquenchable hunger for Mac's death. She desired it beyond all others and she would savour it.

Ultraviolet took the corner into another hallway and

felt something hit her feet. Time slowed as she glanced down. She had stepped on a wire running across the hall's length. Her eyes followed the wire until she saw two grenades duck taped to the wall beside her. It was a booby trap. Whoever stepped on this wire would cause the grenades to detonate and they would explode in the person's face. These were the traps Mac had set up at various entrances to the mess. They were an effective trick for most people but not for a speedster. No human could run fast enough after triggering the trap to escape the blast. She was not a mere human. She was a meta-human. Ultraviolet sped down the hall. She'd escape the frag grenades. Ultraviolet looked down the hallway and saw Mac at the other end, standing there in her shades. Ultraviolet drew her knives and charged at the soldier but as she got closer she realized that Mac was standing there with a smirk on her face and her middle finger extended. Something was wrong. Ultraviolet glanced to the wall and cursed as she saw it. Several flash bangs were duct taped to the wall, each several feet apart and connected to the same wire. The wire wasn't simply triggering the frag grenades - the frags were simply a diversion to force her further into the hall - they were also triggering the flash bangs.

The grenades exploded and filled the hallway with a blinding light. Mac closed her eyes and dove to the side. Ultraviolet slammed into the wall at the end of the hall with a sickening smash. Mac rolled to her side and flipped to her feet. She snapped her rifle up and aimed it at the staggering speedster. Ultraviolet tried to climb to her feet and call upon her speed but quickly found herself falling back to the floor.

A flash bang momentarily activated all photoreceptor cells in the eye. For the next five seconds it made vision impossible. Even after a pair of eyes returned to its normal, unstimulated state, the subject would see an after image. The loud bang also caused a temporary loss of hearing and disturbed the fluid in an ear that caused a loss of balance.

Mac lowered her rifle. She drew her M17 as she walked over to the speedster. She kicked the speedster onto her back. Kaluuya stared up at Mac and her afterimage. Mac stared back.

"You're not the first speedster I've fought," Mac revealed. "What I've learned is speedsters - as a rule - don't think things through. If you can outthink them, you can beat them. I had a six point plan to beat you.

"Point One: get a weapon for DJ. Point Two: booby trap the doors. Point Three: rig this hallway with grenades. Point Four: free the hostages. Point Five: Lure you here. That leaves point six. Any guesses?" Kaluuya tried to get up but Mac slammed her foot into the speedster's chest and forced her back into the floor.

"Point six: put a bullet in your skull." Mac leveled the M17 at Ultraviolet's head. "The Israeli woman didn't deserve what you did to her."

"Savour...my...last...breath."

Mac pulled the trigger.

Phylicia Kaluuya was dead.

CHAPTER 12

Mac dropped to the floor. She landed on her ass with a thud and winced. Her arm and her ribs whimpered slightly. Both were still sore from Morozko and the fall. Mac sighed. She was going to have to face him next. Fighting the bald ice-Russian wasn't going to be easy. He'd already kicked her ass once; luckily Mac was a woman who learned from her mistakes. Marozko was taller and stronger. He towered over her and his punches were like meteorites, crashing down from space. Then there were the ice powers; he was quick with his glacial blasts and ice walls. She was at a disadvantage in medium combat and close-quarter combat. In a perfect world she'd give DJ a sniper rifle and let him put a bullet through Morozko's head at a mile away. Mac silently scolded herself. She couldn't even cherish one victory without worrying about the next fight.

The sound of footsteps caught her attention. Mac rolled to her knees and raised her M4. She stared down the sights and found weapon leveled at DJ. Mac sighed and lowered her weapon. "You okay, boss lady?"

"No lie, I could use Cell right now but I'll be fine." Cell was the group's healer. He could manipulate living tissues - to repair or cause harm - with but a touch. "How are you? How's the neck?"

DJ gently rubbed his neck. Bruises outlined in the shape of a hand were already starting to form on his neck. DJ shook his head. "I don't get the choking kink and today definitely didn't make me want to try it."

"There is a certain appeal to the risk," Mac said. DJ eyed her and Mac just smirked. DJ rolled his eyes. She was bullshitting him, she had to be. "How are the rest of the people in there?"

"Many of them are scared but they still want to take the base back by force."

"We're not going to do that, not yet," Mac ordered. "Something else is happening here and I don't want them getting caught up in it. This is more than some stupid revenge mission." DJ raised an eye. Mac quickly explained.

"Thanatos? Isn't that your Dad?"

"My Old Man," Mac corrected. "Yeah, that's him, but if they want revenge there are much simpler ways to get it."

"What's our next step?"

"I'm heading to the lab next," Mac explained. "But I'm waiting to see what Zetes digs up first."

Mac glanced at the speedster's corpse. Kaluyya may have more yet to say. Mac knelt by the body and started digging through the pockets. She pulled out a familiar radio and tossed it to DJ. He caught it easily. Mac dug out a phone. She pressed Kaluyya's finger against the sensor and watched it unlock. She handed it to DJ and asked him to go through it. Mac pulled free a folded piece of paper. She unfolded it and saw several familiar numbers.

- ~~14015~~
- ~~14112~~
- 14180
- 14025 - boss
- ~~14252~~

Several numbers were scratch out and one had the word boss written beside it in pen. Mac frowned. Operators like Mac and the Death Hounds were trained to memorize numbers. They weren't supposed to keep them written down for the literal reason that they were now in Mac's hands. How many sources were trying to contact agents that they couldn't remember them all? Mac was tired of reacting. It was time to force the Death Hounds to react to her. Mac grabbed the radio and punched in 14025. A couple seconds later a familiar voice came across it.

"Is Mac dead?"

"Not yet, Shatalov," Mac replied. "I'm still here and kicking."

"Where's Kaluuya?"

"Right beside Orman," Mac mocked. "They're both fucking dead."

Silence.

"I think it's about time you pack it in, Shatalov. You don't want me to kill anybody else do you? Go home and get your Daddy to tuck you into bed before I have to come up there and kill you as well." Mac wanted to put Shatalov off her guard. She wanted her to start making mistakes. "Oh wait, Daddy can't tuck you in can he? In fact the entire reason you're here is because Daddy ate a bullet, isn't it?"

"I will kill you, Mac."

"Your speedster said something similar to me," Mac explained. "I shot her. Now listen up because I'm only going to say this once. I'm coming for you now. I'm coming across this base and into the lab and I'm going to kill you. So take every soldier you have and put them in the lab. Put each and every one of your Whitestar assholes on guard duty because then maybe - just maybe - you'll survive meeting me face to face."

"I still have Blindspot," Shatalov laughed. "You wouldn't dare risk his life."

"Agent: Blindspot is the only reason I've held back today. Just imagine the mad dog I'll become without the leash holding me back." Mac shut off the radio.

"Brilliant, just brilliant." DJ started a slow clap. Mac turned towards her friend and gave him an eye. "The Oscar goes to you. That was some epic level taunting." Mac just smirked in return.

"You ready?" DJ checked his weapon. He nodded. "Good, let's go find a fight."

Einin Moran sat in a chair, her eyes locked onto the face of Agent: Blindspot. She didn't look at the rest, she simply stared at him. She stared at him with hurt and anger in her eyes. Gunner recognized the look. She had just lost someone and didn't know what to do. She wanted to blame everybody, to lash out at anybody she could all for that brevity of release.

"Just tell her how to unlock it," Einin said suddenly. "More don't have to die for you stubbornness. They killed my brother over this, over you."

"Fuck you," Blindspot said. "Your brother deserved to ---"

A fist slammed against his face. Einin stood before him, having leapt from her chair. She stood over the Tier 4 manager, rage filling her eyes. "Everybody that dies here today is on you. Every one of our soldiers and every one of yours; their deaths will weigh on your shoulders."

The doors opened and Shatalov walked in. She took one look at Einin and started yelling. "What the fuck are you doing in here?" Einin tried to respond but Shatalov never gave her the chance. "Get the fuck out of this room and find out where the fuck Mac is."

"My powers don't work well in the camp," Einin explained. "It's unlikely that I could find her."

"Well how about you *fucking try*!" Shatalov screamed.

Einin nodded and dashed out of the room. Shatalov stole glance at Gunner before leaving herself. Gunner's eyes followed her and watched, through the glass, as she kicked a chair and slammed her radio on the table. Shatalov was angry because things weren't going according to plan. That meant Mac was winning. Gunner smirked. He was proud of his girl.

Gunner eyes moved to Lt. Latif. The Lieutenant was Shatalov's second in command. The 2IC had a massive beard and dozens of muscles. He kept a blade at close reach which meant he was a knife aficionado. Gunner hated knife aficionados. Yet what really bothered him was his stance. Every military *basically* trained their soldiers in the same way but there still were differences. Each group tended to hold themselves differently. Each stood slightly different. It was a body-language signature for their training. Latif wasn't Spetnaz or SEALs. He wasn't ARW, Jagdkommando or Kommando Spezialkräfte. What was he? Gunner's face went white. Suddenly he recognized the stance. He was JTF2. Lt. Latif was a god damn Canadian. Gunner silently cursed. The worst fight he ever had was against a Canadian. He was a former member of the Airborne who had been assigned elsewhere after the regiment was disbanded. Gunner hated fighting Canadians. Those canucks knew how to take a fucking punch and how to throw one. The worst part was after they kicked his ass, they apologized. Fucking Canadians, they weren't human.

"You're doing a real shitty job of protecting me, Guns," Blindspot said as he spat blood onto the floor.

"I keep telling you, Dale, I'm not a bodyguard," Gunner smirked, looking back at his friend. "You're the one who chose me for this mission."

"I won't make *that* mistake again," Dale said with a nervous laugh. Gunner frowned. He glanced at his friend and gave him a stern look.

"I need an answer, a real one," Gunner said. "Does this have to do with South America?"

"Yes."

"You're still working on that?" Gunner said with a shake of his head. "I thought that it was dead in the water?"

"Not anymore, Guns." Agent: Blindspot let out a small smirk. "I found my missing link. I got it to work. Project: Nestor was a success."

Mac's rifle roared to life. She fired in controlled bursts, her grip never loosening and her aim never faltering. She simply kept her arms firm, her breathing steady and kept firing. DJ bolted past Mac and charged into the room, his rifling firing as he ran. The two had fought beside each other enough times to know how the other thought and reacted. The pair, despite being teammates, couldn't have had more different styles if they tried. Mac moved like a machine, picking off problems before they arose and using cover as needed. DJ ran into battle and moved like a dancing dervish. When DJ fought he let his hearing go to max. His ears would catch every detail. He could hear the next round being forced into the chamber, he could hear the strain a finger put on the trigger and he could hear the shift in the wind as a bullet tore towards him. DJ heard it all and reacted. He'd shift his body and the bullet would pass by harmlessly. He would pivot and a bullet would hit the wall instead of him. He would suddenly point his rifle in a seemingly random direction and fire and someone would fall over, dead. DJ heard it all.

As the final soldier fell, DJ and Mac came to a halt. DJ's chest heaved as he panted for air but Mac's barely moved. DJ raised an eyebrow. A smile crept across his lips.

"You have super endurance," he laughed.

"What?"

"Your power. The power that none of us have been able to guess until now, it's super endurance." He whooped. "That's why nobody has seen it since now. You've always used the power. It's why you're barely out of breath and I'm exhausted."

"It's not super endurance," Mac said with a roll of her eyes. "You're out of breath because you're out of shape. You gave up on your cardio training."

DJ frowned. He hated cardio training. He hated when Mac was right.

The pair looked around the building. They weren't in the lab, they were in the armoury. The ambush was gone and only a few guards remained. Shatalov had pulled most of the guards from the building to protect the lab. Mac smiled. How many times was Shatalov going to fall for that trick?

"Gear up," Mac ordered.

Mac walked towards the gun vault and smashed open the lock. She kicked open the door and marched in. Mac froze as she eyed the arsenal. She shook her head in confusion. She eyed the dozens of M4s, the M249s, the various grenade launchers and anti-tank weapons. She called DJ in.

"What's up?" DJ asked as he walked in. He froze and took a look around. "Holy hell, look at this place. Why the fuck do they have so many weapons?"

"I have no clue." The rifles, shotguns and pistols made sense but the grenade launchers, light machine guns and the *anti-tank* weapons? There was no reason in hell a small science base should have that type of arsenal. "What the fuck are they making here?"

"I don---" DJ words suddenly cut off. He walked directly to the sniper rifles and picked up a M110. "Hello, beautiful."

The M110 was a sandy brown coloured semi-automatic sniper rifle with a gas-operated rotating bolt. It had a maximum range of nearly 1200 yards. This rifle was far from being his Baby. That honour went to his highly customized Denel NTW-20. Yet despite their differences, the M110 would be perfect for this mission. DJ quickly ran his hands over the weapon, thoroughly checking each part before moving onto the next. He ignored the weapon's sights. He rarely used them anyways.

Mac started by grabbing grenades. She pocketed the frag grenades, the flash bangs and grabbed several smoke grenades to add to her arsenal. She grabbed two boxes of 5.56 ammo and stared to refill her empty magazines.

"Raven this is Zetes."

"Go for Raven."

"I----ning to ---- hold." Static filled the line. "Channel Switch."

Mac smirked. She knew what Zetes was doing. Zetes was covertly trying to get her to switch channels so they could speak privately. It was standard procedure for her team. When things didn't add up, they played it close to the chest. Mac flicked to the secondary channel.

"Go for Raven."

"I did some digging around," Zetes said, "and I'm coming up short on the details. This Morrell Blood operation is black bag, even within the company."

"That's just great," Mac mumbled.

"The base uses the Lepton VR system and genetic experimentation to activate the Lycotta gene." The Lepton VR system was *supposed* to help train soldiers. Instead it was used to simulate near-death experience in order to trigger a meta-change. "The base also has a secret objective. This base was built for Project: Nestor."

"I don't know much about Project: Nestor but Agent: Blindspot has been trying to get approval for the base for the last ten years. He has been denied every time, until last year. I don't know what he did to change things, but he got approval.

"Nobody seems to know anything about Nestor and those who do aren't talking. All I know is it has to do with a 2006 mission in South America. Blindspot was low level management at the time. He's spent the last ten years climbing the ladder. Something happened in South America, Raven, something involving your--- the old man."

2006? South America? Mac frowned. Would that weekend never cease to stop haunting her?

"This is worse than it sounds, Raven. If I couldn't find out about this there is no way Whitestar could either," Zetes said. Mac knew he wasn't bragging, Zetes could find anything out about anybody given enough time. "There is someone playing both sides in this."

"What are the numbers we're talking about?" Mac asked. "How many people could have known about this base? We have entire divisions of people who build bases and secure areas. That doesn't count the set-up crew or the legal division. There could be hundreds who know of this base."

"True but you said they're after Project: Nestor specifically. That seriously limits the numbers." Zetes went quiet for a moment. "That means our traitor is either high management - which is unlikely -, part of the science division in Morrell Blood - who are all hostages at this moment - or they were part of Ops' logistical teams."

Logistical teams? Mac growled. She was hoping it wasn't the case, she was hoping that her darker instincts were just the by-product of a paranoid fueled life but it quickly proving not to be the case. Things were starting to add up. They knew about Gunner and were trying to draw him out. Mac had already proved there was a leak and now she wondered if both were connected to the traitor. Mac had her suspicions. There was one who had gone out of his way to restrict Mac's access to intel.

Grammer Ford.

Keane grabbed the kid out of logistics. He would have access to the base's intel and probably even helped in setup. He would have been the few to know of Morrell Blood's true purpose. There was only one way to find out.

Mac reached into her vest and pulled free a piece of folded paper. She opened it up and stared once more at the list of codes she had taken from Ultraviolet's body. 14180: the number had shown up on several lists. It had showed up enough times to be important. Mac grabbed her stolen radio and thumbed in the number. There was only one way to find out what it meant.

"Here goes nothing," Mac said to Zetes before switching to her stolen radio.

"What do you need?" Mac blinked in surprise. That voice on the line wasn't Grammer Ford's. That voice was one she recognized very well. It was a voice she trusted.

"Wesley Keane?" asked in shock. Mac repeated the name, this time with a deep angry growl. "Wesley Keane, you traitorous son of a bitch!"

Then the line went silent.

CHAPTER 13

Agent Grammer Ford hated being behind a desk. He was a field agent, always had been and always would be. Sadly, fate had other plans. One rogue telepath and he was benched forever. Ford hated telepaths, almost as much as he hated being behind a desk.

High above the Alaskan sky flew the *Trautman*. The plane held Ford, Keane, two pilots and two additional support troops. The *Trautman* also held several computers, radio equipment and enough guns to start a small war. It was all nostalgic for Ford. He started many missions on a plane such as this. The only difference was he was normally the one to be leaping out of the plane, not the one impatiently waiting.

Ford twisted the knobs and dials on the radio equipment that sat before him. He was monitoring all channels for incoming or outgoing transmissions. He had easily tracked each of the Death Hound's transmissions but decoding their encryption was a different matter entirely. There had been a couple hidden transmissions but most were too short to track. This one, however, was a rather lengthy one. He scanned channel after channel until he found it.

It was Mac and Zetes. Why were they chatting on a secondary channel? What were they trying to hide? He tuned into the channel and turned up the volume so he could carefully listen.

"This is worse than it sounds, Raven. If I couldn't find

out about this there is no way Whitestar could either," Zetes said over the radio. *"There is someone playing both sides in this."*

There was someone playing both sides? It was possible but unlikely. Ford shook his head. Visegar wasn't free of the internal debates that the various three-letter government agencies dealt with. Its internal struggles tended to be more vicious. Still, how many suspects were there?

"What are the numbers we're talking about?" Mac asked. *"How many people could have known about this base? We have entire divisions of people who build bases and secure areas. That doesn't count the set-up crew or the legal division. There could be hundreds who know of this base."*

Shit. He was right. The numbers were large. Ford's mind raced as he ran through the names he knew. Several came to mind, agents he knew from either the field or logistics, but none seemed to have motive.

"True but you said they're after Project: Nestor specifically. That seriously limits the numbers." Zetes said. *"That means our traitor is either high management - which is unlikely, part of the science division in Morrell Blood - who are all hostages at this moment or they were part of Ops' logistical teams."*

Zetes was smart; Ford had to give the con artist that. He was a quick thinker and a logical one. He had quickly taken a list of nearly two hundred and whittled it down to a generous twenty. Yet his information was lacking. Just because they were part of logistics didn't mean they had access. Ford was a low ranking Logistical member. He had seen the name Project: Nestor, it was on a list of projects that the new base was going to setup, but he knew nothing about it. Information about it was restricted. Only his supervisor, Keane, and Logistical management had access to it.

"Here goes nothing," Mac said.

Two beeps filled the plane. One came from Keane's desk while the other came from the consol before him. Ford looked at his scanner. Another encrypted message was being broadcasted.

"What do you need?" Keane said from across the plane.

"What was that?" Ford asked. He looked back over his shoulder, thinking that Keane was talking to him, and blinked in confusion. Keane was on a secondary radio. He wasn't using the plane's communication systems, he was using a different device altogether. "Sir?"

Keane didn't answer; he was too focused on his radio. Ford pushed back from his console and crept over to his boss. He needed to see what was going on. As he got closer he could hear the voice on the other end of the radio.

"Wesley Keane? Wesley Keane, you traitorous son of a bitch!" That voice was Mac's. Why was she using this radio to talk to Keane instead of her own? It didn't make sense unless....

- Keane had details about Project: Nestor
- Keane had money issues
- Keane had a bone to pick with Ops.
- Keane had a hidden radio

Mac was right, Keane was the traitor.

"Step away from the desk, sir." Keane turned around and saw Ford standing behind him, a gun in his hand. "You've been relieved of duty."

"What the hell are you talking about?" Keane said, his voice shaking with each word. Keane's mind raced as he tried to figure a way out of this. Ford knew the man was swift and clever. He knew that he had to keep focused.

"Step away from the desk, sir. Don't make me shoot you."

You wouldn't shoot that in here," Keane said with a weak laugh. "You could kill us all if you did."

"Step away, final warning."

Keane lunged at Ford, hoping to take the kid down, but he never even reached him. Ford pulled the trigger and

Keane paid the price. He didn't hear a bang or felt the cold touch a bullet made when it came into contact with skin; instead he heard a buzz and felt several seconds' worth of electricity pumping into his chest. Ford wasn't holding a gun, he was holding a taser. Keane screamed as he hit the floor. His body violently twitched, eventually falling still.

"What the hell?" one of the additional support troops asked, his hand dropping to the weapon on his belt.

"What's going on back there?" the pilot yelled from the cockpit.

"He's trying to get Mac killed." Ford reloaded his taser, speaking quickly as he did. "He's feeding the terrorist intel and even help them set up an ambush. He fucking sold us out."

The soldier eyed Keane and Ford, unsure of what to do. The co-pilot emerged from the cockpit with a SIG Sauer in his hand. He looked at both men and then nodded to the soldier. "Secure Keane and then we'll figure this out."

The soldier zipped Keane' hands together and dragged him to a nearby chair. Ford bolted for Keane's radio. Mac was still on the line. She needed an update. He grabbed it and thumbed it on.

"Raven, this is *Trautman*. Switch to normal channels."

"Confirmed." For dropped Keane's radio back onto the table and moved to the plane's radio desk. He switched to their main channel. Mac's voice came across. "Go for Raven."

"Keane's been removed from command," Ford explained. "As of right now I am *Trautman* Actual."

"What the fuck is happening up there, Actual?"

"I have no clue," Ford admitted. "I'm going to find out. Mission parameters would suggest you hold position until I can determine the damage Keane has caused."

"Negative, Actual," Mac said. "We don't have the time to play wait and see. I'm proceeding with the objective."

Mac scooped up her ammo and quickly pocketed them. She grabbed her rifle and turned towards DJ. The sniper caressed his newly acquired weapon like a single woman caressed her cat. She didn't need to give the sniper an update; the meta had already heard everything. He always heard everything.

Working with DJ took some getting used to. There were few secrets with a meta who heard everything, especially when she didn't want them to. Throughout her career, Mac had tried to keep her work life separate from her civilian life - what little she had. When Mac had assembled her team, she was mystery to everybody except Rath. She told them little about herself despite knowing almost everything about each of them. DJ didn't like this dynamic. For the man who heard everything, having a secret kept from him did little but engaged his curiosity. DJ tried to learn more about his mysterious leader and it wasn't until he overheard a phone call between Mac and her BFF that he discovered more. Mac was meeting Holly for lunch, so DJ decided to crash the event. Mac was not amused, even less so when DJ started to flirt and hit on Holly. Despite learning he was *barking up the wrong tree* he still hit it off with Holly. The two now did coffee on a regular basis, a fact that still annoyed Mac.

There were no secrets with the man who heard everything.

"You're on overwatch," Mac ordered. "Get to the roof and keep an ear open."

"'Step into my parlor,' said the spider to the fly," DJ said with a wink. He grabbed a bag full of supplies and bolted for the side door. Mac rolled her eyes. She checked her gear one more time before moving to the door. She paused by and waited. Several moments later DJ came across her radio. "I'm in position."

"Roger that." Mac took a deep breath. She steadied her breathing and looked at the door. She quietly muttered to herself. "No time like the present."

"What am I going to do with you, Keane?" Ford asked. He stared at his once-supervisor. He was zipped to a chair. "You know every interrogation tactic that I do. You've been trained to withstand it. The problem is I still need to know what you did and why?"

"Why does it matter?"

"We know you betrayed the company. I've already reported it in. Security is tearing through your systems as we speak." Keane flinched. Ford pressed on. "Why, man, why? What possessed you to switch team?"

Keane shook his head. Ford frowned. He decided to switch tactics. "You were smart to get out of the field when you did. Field work is destructive to our bodies, our minds and our relationships. I know things aren't great with your wife right now, I know you two are separated, but at least you get to be home to fix it."

"We're not separated," Keane admitted. "She left me. She moved out, took our kids and we're going through a massive divorce."

"What about your daughters?"

"She took them from me," he spat. "The bitch took my fucking kids away from me and I can't even afford to fight for them."

"Is this.....is this about money?" Ford asked hesitantly. He was on the verge of something here but if he pressed to hard, Keane would clam up. Keane shook his head.

"It is but it isn't," he admitted. "Field work is shit but it makes sense. You do your job and if you're good enough *not* to die then you get to come home to your kids and family. In the field there are good guys and there are bad guys. There is black and there is white. Back home there is....so much grey. Am I the bad guy for doing my job? My wife thinks so, she says I'm never around and I'm the bad guy because of that. So I left the field. I took a desk job to be with her. What do I get for my effort? I get a shit posting in logistics and I find out that wife can't fucking stand me. But you know what she can stand? She can stand fucking my neighbour, her boss and our daughter's fucking soccer coach. That asshole boy is still in college.

"Whitestar made me an offer: they'd help me get out. They would give me enough money to retire and fight for my daughters. I'd have enough to send my girls to school and make sure they never wanted for anything, ever. They gave me the chance to be the father that I should have been my entire life."

"So you gave them what they wanted."

"I've been feeding them intel for years. Most of the time it was info on bases and projects but this time was different. They told me they were interested in Project: Nestor and they needed info on the base. I didn't even know what Nestor was. When I help set up Morrell Blood I did so with an itemized list of what was needed. I have no clue what the project is. All I know is they want it."

"You were willing to kill Mac to let them get it?"

"It wasn't supposed to be Mac. She was supposed to be on the bodyguard duty with Rath and DJ," Keane said. "He was replaced with Gunner - at Agent: Blindspot's request. This trap was supposed to be for Thanatos."

"Who is Thanatos?"

"Thanatos is a fucking myth," Keane yelled. "He's the meta-world's version of the boogeyman. Shatlov is fucking nuts. She's pissed off that Ops sent Thanatos to kill her dad."

"But Ops didn't send Thanatos," Ford said. "HQ finally gave us access to the Death Hound mission. They sent Gunner."

"Gunner is Thanatos," Keane said in disbelief. "Fucking hell, they already have him."

"They just don't know it's him," Ford finished. He turned away from his one-time boss and stared at the map of Morrell Blood. He shook his head. Mac needed to hurry. Gunner didn't have long to live.

CHAPTER 14

Mac bolted across the yard praying not to die. Between the science building and the armoury was a large open space with little for cover. If the Whitestar goons wanted a shot at her, this was it. Soldiers stood in the building, aiming from open windows or down from the roof. Some patrolled the building's perimeter, looking for any sign of her. The moment one of them saw her, they shifted their aim but none of them got the chance to fire.

DJ lay prone on the armoury rooftop. He closed his eyes and let the reach of his hearing expand. Thousands of auditory details flooded his mind, each adding to an image that formed in his mind. The image in his mind was greater than what his eyes could create. DJ could see each soldier and he knew the exact moment when each of them shifted their aim, when they squeezed the trigger and when their hearts beat faster at the moment they intended to fire. Each detail was like a highlighted paragraph in a book. It was impossible to miss.

- Third Floor: Eastern window
- Ground: Two men on patrol
- Roof: Center with a downward aim

DJ body moved quickly. One after another his rifle moved and fired. Each shot locked onto the body of a potential threat against Mac and a placed a 7.62×51mm NATO round through their chest. Four shots rang out and four men dropped. DJ's hearing expanded again.

- Second Floor: Two men approach windows
- Roof: Two more running to the edge
- Ground: One man hiding behind the science building's doors

DJ shifted his body as he aimed again. He squeezed off two rounds. Each ripped through glass and dove into the target's body. A quick shift and DJ fired twice. Two more rounds ripped through the air and dove into chest of two unsuspecting soldiers who had just reached the roof's edge. DJ shifted his aim once more and lined his rifle up with the lab's doors. He fired a fifth round and smiled as it dove down from above and punched down through the door and into the neck of a very startled soldier. DJ smiled. He was *really* good at his job.

Mac kicked open the science building's door and entered rifle first. Her aim moved with her eyes as Mac scanned the entrance. She heard a sound and both snapped to her left. Her gaze fell on the forms of two hidden soldiers. They popped up from their cover with hopes of gunning her down. They never got the chance. Mac's shots were quick with a tight grouping. She dropped both in half a second. Mac pushed herself forward. Her body still stung with pain but she ignored it. Pain was a luxury and not one she could afford at the moment.

Mac moved quickly and carefully. She paused at a corner, checked it and moved on. Any soldier she came across quickly fell to her gunfire. This had been a long day for her and it had taken its toll on her body, her mind and her patience. The first casualty of this was her hesitance to kill. Not every soldier she came across received a killing blow, some were lucky enough to be shot in the shoulder or the leg. Some would survive if they were tended to soon enough and others would have to scramble not to bleed out. But Mac was no longer worried about her kill count. She worried only about saving the hostages. The fate of the terrorist had already been decided the moment they took the base. Those who survived the day were on borrowed time.

The science building was varied. Some floors and offices dealt with the VR training. Others tested plants unique to the Tongass National Forest for their medical benefit. Each of the experiments looked to strengthen a human or to exploit the Lycotta gene. Then there was Project: Nestor

Mac crept into the inner laboratory and looked around. The majority of the second floor was reserved for Project: Nestor. Mac pushed open the emergency doors and crept inwards. The second floor was filled with smaller labs, each working on an aspect of Nestor. Mac moved through the floor. She paused by one door and glanced in. She saw several glass chambers filled with dirt, grass and ants. Each container was a large and fully functional ant farm with dozens of sensors and various pieces of equipment monitoring it at all times. Mac moved down the long grey hallway and paused at another door. With a glance inside she saw several stirrup chairs. They were the type of chair a woman sat in when she went to the gynaecologist. A shiver ran down Mac's spine as she tried to envision herself in that chair with the ant-room right down the hall. Mac walked further. She glanced in several other doors and saw dozens of pieces of equipment, most of which she couldn't begin to name. Mac paused at one of the offices and silently let herself in. She sat down behind the computer. She removed her rifle from around her neck and leaned it against the desk. Then she removed her pistol and placed it atop the desk, beside the laptop. She wanted quick access to the weapon if someone came stumbling in.

Mac's fingers quickly danced across the keyboard. The computer's security provided little in the way of resistance. Mac was a Visegar Operative. She knew how to quickly gain access to any Visegar system. She tabbed through the menu and started searching the servers for any mention of Nestor. A series of files came up. Mac started skimming them, one after another, but most of the technical and medical writing was *way* beyond her comprehension. Mac was far from an idiot but when it came to the sciences, she was a dud. Mac saw several video journal entries and tapped on one. A garnet haired woman appeared on the screen. She was older and wore glasses. Mac recognized her at the woman Gunner was hitting on. Mac tapped the mouse and the video started playing. Mac watched for several moments and shut it off. It was a day to day journal and she didn't have to follow it. Mac was about to abandon the journals when she saw a second file with five different journals. Mac opened the file and played the first.

"My name is Dr. Joni Polito," the woman began. She sat in the very chair that Mac was currently in. She looked at a camera and spoke. "I am the lead scientist on Project: Nestor. I was assigned to this project after my success with other endeavours. To be honest, I thought I was going to lose out on this position to Dr. Madison Harper.

"My primary journals are recorded and filed as per normal. These are my secondary recordings. These are my.... reservations and concerns I have with the project. My words won't make a difference but I need them heard. I need them known. I have done a lot in my life that people would look down on me for. I have done a lot of things that I am not proud of. I have manipulated and used people. I have betrayed friends who both trusted and looked up to me. I have tortured metas and put people through incomparable pain and agony. I do this because I belief that the ends *does* justify the means. The advances we have made in medical science and the tens of thousands of lives we've saved far outweigh the hundreds whose lives I've ruined. I'm a scientist and science exists on numbers. But this....this goes too far, especially after the *Formica incident.*

"In 2006, Agent: Blindspot was visiting a company outpost in South America. They were examining wildlife and foliage native to the rainforest. Among the new discoveries was a new breed of ant discovered by an Entomologist named Dr. Christian Arvizu. The new breed was originally mistaken as an existing one but they were quickly corrected. Dr. Arvizu took several ants and began to study them. The colony didn't like this. There is still much of what happened that day that we don't know but as best as the company figures, the ants thought they were being attacked and decided to retaliate in an effort to protect themselves. It started with several large enraged animals who charged into the base, seemingly at random. Then the ants attacked themselves.

"The new breed - *Formica Superior* - is a strain of ant that is blessed with a hive mind. This wasn't swarm intelligence or an apparent consciousness of the colony. This was a true-blue hive mind. This was Unity. This was Jasmine. This was the Borg. The queen was in control and the rest shared a mind. So when Arvizu started experimenting on the new ants, the entire colony felt it. Worse still, each warrior ant carried with it a venom that when inserted into an organism could force that creature - albeit temporarily - into their queen's hive. They forced the animals to attack and then they stormed the base. They swarmed a soldier with hundreds of ants and they filled his body with the venom. One of the other soldiers said in his report that 'it was like the beetles in that Mummy flick.'

"The incident was resolved primarily due to the actions of an unknown agent who was there accompanying visiting members. Several lives were lost - including Arvizu's - but Agent: Blindspot saw potential in the insect. With a new team of Entomologists they took several ants and started cultivating several colonies of their own." Polito shook her head. "Project: Nestor is our attempt to build a hive mind. The worst part of it, we're going to succeed at doing it."

Mac stared at the screen for a moment. She could hear the remorse in Polito's voice and she could see the fear in her eyes. The Doctor was scared of Nestor. A hive mind, was it really possible? Mac had thought herself done asking that question, she had seen enough to know that anything was possible, but the words still hung in her mind. Mac tapped the second video. Dr. Polito reappeared on the screen. This time she looked tired.

"Scientists are geeks. This should come as no surprise to anyone here. For half of us, it was shows like *Star Trek* that got us into our various fields of science." The doctor grabbed a black mug off of her desk and took a sip. Her face scrunched up as she realized that the coffee within was cold. With a tired expression she shrugged and downed the cold coffee. "For me it was the films of Roger Corman. I never knew why but I loved his work. *Deathrace 2000, Machine-Gun Kelly, Grand Theft Auto* and *Rock 'n' Roll High School*, I saw them all but it was the sci-fi movies that touched me. *Forbidden World, Galaxy of Terror, It Conquered the World* and, my personal favourite, *Battle Beyond the Stars*; I devoured them, over and over." She took another sip of her cold coffee. "What is it about movies that link people together? Is it the communal viewing in a theatre? Or is it the shared experience we all have at different times and places? Sometimes I wonder, with all that I've done, if I have lost my humanity? Are movies my only link to what I once was? Are movies the only way in which I can still feel?

"I gave Nestor its name. I was its creator, I was its mother. Our goal was to recreate the *Formica Superior*'s ability to link and control others in a hive. We started by examining the ant's venom but this led to difficulties. The venom is primarily used to dominate workers from rival colonies and steal them away. The *Formica Superior* has also shown skill at dominating the minds of larger creature. They can't make them join the hive but they can enrage the creature enough to attack, as they saw in South America. The venom wasn't potent enough to tackle a human mind. This was the first problem we had. The second issue was there was no *host* for the venom. We needed more venom and we needed a queen. Our solution of both came from a remarkable source: cancer." Dr. Polito reached for the keyboard to halt the recording but her arm paused in mid air. A concerned look crossed her face. "What will happen when Roger Corman dies? What will I be like then?"

The second video came to a halt. It was obvious that Polito was recording these video after the fact, like she was looking back on the events that had happened and questioning her decisions. Mac quickly tapped on the third. Dr. Polito reappeared on the screen. She looked even more tired than before. It was like she had lost the ability to sleep.

"When I was twelve years old, I told my father that I wanted to be a doctor. He smiled and told me that if I was going to be a doctor, I would have to save the world. He told me that he wouldn't accept anything less than the best. My father was a man's man. He worked hard in a factory, drank, smoked and never settled for second best on anything. I was twenty-one when he died of cancer. I cried for a week. Three years ago I lost my second husband to cancer. I didn't feel a thing. Do other people mean so little to me now?

"Bridgette Ryman was dying of lung cancer before she came to us. I don't know what lie her and her FBI brother were told but it was all bullshit. We can't cure her, not even slightly, but we can make her life a living hell. Cancer is the abnormal cell growth inside a human body. We wanted to harness that growth." Dr. Polito was fidgety. She's scratched her arm and her neck with each passing moment. She looked like an addict, desperate for a fix.

"Ms. Ryman was at one of our *actual* cancer trials for several years. We moved her here because of the unique nature of her cancer. Bridgette had a high Lycotta count yet she had no signs of powers. It turned out her power was adaptation. Her body was trying to adapt and change to protect itself. When she came here we wanted to use that power to help grow a new synthetic batch of venom.

"I tortured that woman for months as I tried to control how her body changed. Every waking moment of hers was filled with unbearable pain. Ms. Ryman's life was a waking nightmare. I cut her open and stitched her back together, I fried her skin and nearly flayed her alive. But it was all worth it because eventually the body adapted in a way I wanted and her tumour mutated, bonding with the synthetic venom." Polito held up a small vial full of blue liquid. "This is the Formica Coerulus solution but we just call it Blue Ant. God help us if Oversight figures out what we've done."

Mac quickly tapped on the fourth video. Polito looked worse. Large black bags hung beneath her eyes and her entire face seemed to droop. Her eyes were bloodshot and her arms seemed to twitch even more. Mac tapped play.

"The organization I work for is powerful and does a lot of good. It is also toxic. It eats people up and uses them. It drains them of everything good and leaves an empty husk in its wake. For my organization, I have done so much wrong. I have tortured people, I have ripped them down and I have cast them out. I have betrayed some friends and forced others to suicide. Working for the organization is like being in an abusive relationship. It's great if you are in charge but if you're not, then things go bad. They will abuse you, they will emotionally assault you time and time again and then, when you've finally cracked, broken down and fallen into depression, they will cast you out. The organization is toxic and I'm a willing part of it.

"Our first test with Blue Ant was rocky at best. We used it to link the minds of two men together. For a moment it was glorious. They described shared memories and thoughts. From the way they spoke it reminded me of the drift from *Pacific Rim*. Subject Alpha was a soldier. Subject Bravo was an accountant. Both men were going strong for nearly two hours. They showed shared knowledge. Subject Bravo showed a newly obtained skill with firearms and military procedure. Subject Alpha was able to complete several advanced accounting tests we concocted for him. It was during a down period that we saw the test take a turn. Subject Alpha began having difficulties differentiating his memories from those of Bravo's. He descended into what can only be called an existential crisis. He kept asking what was real and what wasn't. He became violent and tried to kill his handler. Ironically, Bravo kept his calm. The accountant subdued a guard, stole his sidearm and then killed Alpha with no hesitation." A tired smile crossed her lips. "It was glorious. I expected someone to snap but I had expected it to be Bravo. I expected him to snap under the pressure and go violent. I wanted to see how he would fair, a man with no training who was linked to a seasoned soldier. But he didn't. The damn fool kept his calm. All of my hypotheses were shattered. It was a moment of pure scientific wonder."

She leaned back in her chair and ran her hand through her hair. A small chuckle emerged followed by what could only be considered a sinister smile. She was remembering that moment with such fondness. It made Mac uneasy. Polito sat up once more.

"Subject Bravo has become a husk of what he once was. He acts like a grieving spouse, walking around like something is missing. He does his daily accounting duties but he's also taken up soldiering. Every morning he joins the soldiers for PT, which is hard to imagine because Bravo is overweight. He was not an active person but now he trains. We have tried this test with ten other pairs. Each time the result was similar; one of the pair would snap and become violent. The survivor would struggle with a void in its life. Most of the ten survivors simply took their own lives while the others became comatose husks. Bravo is the only exception.

"Security is a must here. If Oversight was to find out what we were doing here, their response would be swift. There would be no negotiation and there would be no agent sent in to stop us. They would simply bomb us from above and burn the base to the ground. They would kill us all rather than risk a meta-hive mind onto the world." Once again her hand paused as she tried to stop her recording. "Why did Subject: Bravo fair better than the rest of the survivors? Was it because he's a loser who wanted nothing more than to be John McClane or James Bond? Or is Bravo *just* special?"

Mac stared at the still screen and frowned. Dr. Polito was right, Oversight would bomb the living shit out of Morrell Blood if they found out what was going on here. It was the last thing Visegar wanted. Mac tapped the final journal.

"The day I have long feared has arrived. Project: Nestor is a success." Dr. Polito looked like a different woman. She was relaxed and had slept for what must have been a week. She drank coffee once again but warm this time. "Our success was based on us conquering two major hurdles. The first was the instability of the linked minds and the second was the creation of the venom. We couldn't continue to drain venom from Ms. Ryman mutated tumours. It wasn't feasible. What we needed was a way to produce it ourselves so we could use to ensnare new *ants*. We also needed a *queen ant* for our new *ants* to obey. Our answer came from a video game. We used a virus to bond Blue Ant to a host. The t-Virus, we built our solution around the goddamn t-Virus." Polito let out a small chuckle before taking another sip of coffee. "Technically, according to my team, since it's a double-stranded RNA virus which acts as a high potent non-carcinogenic mutagen we based our solution on the Progenitor virus, not the t-Virus but at this point it doesn't matter.

"Animal testing has proven a great success. Whichever rat is injected with Nestor becomes the *queen* or the center of the hive. Those that are infected afterwards become submissive to their new *queen*. There are few side-effects, the most obvious is that their skin turns blue, but aside from that we have no major meltdowns. Having a dedicated *queen* solved the issues of our previous mind-link. The Nestor virus also allowed for the infected bodies to now produce their own venom.

"An interesting observation of the rats has led me to conclude that a queen's position isn't permanent. We have seen rat-queens being forced into submission by their rat-ants. Assumedly, one with a stronger will can take the throne. I don't know if this is a communal decision amongst the colony or if a second force rises up to challenge the original." Polito took in a big breath and let out a large sigh. "We want to progress to human trials but not without the company's approval. The project's originator, Agent: Blindspot, will be here in a couple days to do an inspection. If successful then we can move onto the next stage. It's a risky step. If a Tier 4 manager is seen by Oversight flying to the Tongass forest in butt-fuck nowhere, Alaska, it will draw suspicion.

"This brings me to my fear. Project: Nestor is nearly complete. Now I am left wondering about the future. What will become of my creation? Will Visegar use it wisely? Will they use it to better mankind or will they use it for power? I fear it's the latter. They will use it for war and power. They will use it as a weapon and not as a tool. Imagine if dozens of men and women - doctors and scientists - lived in a hive mind. Imagine the wonder and greatness they could achieve. Would it be worth it? Would sacrificing the free will - if you believe in such a thing - of a hundred people be worth the thousands or millions you could affect?"

Mac stared at the screen. A look of disbelief hung on her face. They had done it; they had made a hive mind. Mac quietly cursed. What the fuck was Visegar thinking? In what world was a hive mind a good idea. Worse yet, what the fuck were Whitestar and Shatalov going to do with it?

Things started to fall into place. This wasn't about revenge. This was about power. Revenge was the red herring. Shatalov knew if she simply barged into Morrell Blood and went directly for Nestor that Visegar would send every soldier they had to stop them. But if they used a fake unit name, one that would send up red flags, then Ops would approach the situation cautiously. They would send an agent in to investigate. Ops would take their time because Ops wanted answers. The Death Hounds were dead, Rhys Polson knew this as a fact, but in a world with super-healers and men who could fire eye-beams, Whitestar could plant *just enough* doubt into Palson's mind to make him hesitate. Drawing Gunner out was a diversion. If Shatalov actually killed him it would be little more than a bonus for her. Her main goal was Nestor.

Dr. Joni Polito was right about one thing, Oversight would not respond well if they learned about Project: Nestor but Oversight had to know. Mac had to tell them. She reached to her radio and thumbed to a separate channel. This wasn't the channel she shared with Grammer and it wasn't the channel she shared with her team. This was another channel, a highly encrypted channel.

"Radio check," Mac said quickly.

"Locked and secure," a voice replied on the other end. "This is Oversight. Identify yourself."

"This is Legion," Mac said. "I have a situation to report."

CHAPTER 15

Gunner couldn't help but smile as the wind blew across his face. He gripped the handlebars of his Harley and gave the panhead engine a rev. He sped along the county road with Mac following closely behind. Gunner drove a 1978 Harley-Davidson Panhead while Mac rode a Harley-Davidson 1130 V-Rod. Both raced across the country side, happily avoiding both work and the world.

Mac was happy for the escape. Work was trying to say the least. Her last mission was bad, very bad. Too many lives had been lost and not all were deserving of the loss. There was innocent blood on her hands and Mac was struggling to get it off. Sleep had proven elusive. Every time she closed her eyes she saw the bodies. They were strewn about, burned and dismembered because of the air strike that *she'd* ordered. Those lives were on her hands, they were on her consciousness. Gunner waved Mac to the side and both bikes pulled over.

"Is your back acting up, Old Man?" Mac teased. "I mean your back is as old as that bike."

"This bike is from *Every Which Way but Loose*," Gunner protested. Mac rolled her eyes. She never understood Gunner's fascination with gear-flicks. How many times had she'd been made to watch *Vanishing Point, Easy Rider, Cannonball Run, Ronin, Blues Brothers* and both versions *Gone in Sixty Seconds*? If it was a movie about cars and chases, Gunner loved it.

"Let's eat," Gunner said as he detached the satchel from his bike. He walked up a grassy hill and took a seat. Mac nodded quickly and joined him. Gunned pulled out two sandwiches and handed one to his girl. Mac thanked him and the two wordlessly ate. Eventually he turned to his girl and spoke. "That was a rough one."

"Yeah." It was a one-word answer but it spoke volumes. Her last mission had her dealing with a man whose body produced anthrax. It was a fucked up meta-power but worse still he had already accidently killed a dozen people with it. The more scared he got the more anthrax he produced. With each passing minute another person died. They had no option but to order an air-strike on the small European hotel he was in.

"There was no win for that scenario," Gunner explained. Mac just nodded. She knew that but it was of little help.

"I want out," she said.

"I know," Gunner responded.

"I just can't do this anymore," Mac admitted. "Visegar is bad. They do bad things. Why are we fighting to protect them? I've been thinking about this for a while. Why am I protecting an evil corporation? I started doing this because of you, Old Man. I did this because I lo..." She bit back on the words. She couldn't say them, not even now. "I did this because I owe you but I can't do this anymore."

"If you want out, you have my support," Gunner said. "You don't owe me anything, Kiddo. You've never owed me."

"You adopted me, you looked after me," Mac protested.

"I was happy to do," Gunner said with a smile. "Besides, you looked after me as much as I looked after you. I'm just happy that you started having your periods before I showed up because I have no clue how I would have do *that* talk."

"You would have asked whichever of my teachers

you were fucking at that moment to give me the talk," Mac accused with a smile. Gunner smiled back. Mac's smile faded as she spoke. "Why do you do this? Why protect Visegar?"

"What are the three factions?" Gunner asked. Mac eyed him quizzically. Gunner egged her on to answer. With a sigh she spoke.

"Visegar, Polaris and Oversight," she said.

"Good. Now what do you know about Oversight?"

"They watch over the other two companies to make sure that the meta-secret remains a secret. They are the big scary Father in the meta world."

"Exactly but did you know that Oversight isn't the threat Visegar thinks it is?" Gunner asked. "Visegar is massive. It has more resources than Oversight. Polaris has more resources than Oversight. If either went to war against Oversight, the big scary Father would be destroyed."

"Then why does Visegar fear them?"

"While their pockets are smaller, Oversight's reach is longer. They have hands everywhere and they always seem to have the best ear to whisper in. Oversight is feared because they play the game better. They have agents everywhere." Gunner took a bite of his sandwich. "Fifty years ago Oversight created Legion program. Its goal was to put double-agents inside both companies. They would have soldiers and spies watching Visegar from *within* Visegar. These spies would be many, they would be Legion.

"Almost twenty-five years ago I was approached by a man named Coriolanus Redgrave. He saw the training that my Dad gave me and saw my career as a Ranger. He offered me a job within Visegar. It wasn't until I was balls deep that I learned the truth. He offered me to join Legion and I accepted. Since then I have been Legion. I go on missions for Visegar and then Legion gives me a counter-mission. I have failed main missions for Visegar because I was doing what was *right* for Legion and the public."

Mac stared in silence. A small spark of hope glimmered inside of her. Gunner wasn't the man she thought he was. He didn't fight for Visegar, he fought for Legion. He fought for the people. Mac smiled.

"Coriolanus Redgrave?" Gunner nodded. "That name sounds *really* fake."

"I said the *exact* same thing to his face when I met him," Gunner laughed.

"So tell me more," Mac said, "about this Legion."

"How bad is the threat, Legion?" the Oversight agent asked.

"It's a Level 2 threat," Mac replied.

"Confirm: Level 2 threat?" he asked in disbelief. Oversight ranked threats on their severity. Level 5 was the lowest threat. Level 1 meant a global meta-catastrophe was imminent.

"Threat confirmed."

"Hold." The line went silent for several moments. The operator was not cleared to handle Level 2 threats. They had to be handled by someone with more seniority. A new voice came on the line.

"Legion, this is Ice Pick." Mac recognized the name and the voice. This was Tyrone Straub. He was a senior agent. "What is the threat?"

"We have an armed military incursion from Whitestar onto a hidden Visegar base," Mac began. "The real threat is that Visegar has been working on a hive mind virus. It had a major threat of getting free and spreading."

"A hive mind? Shit," Tyrone said. "We need all the intel you have on the hive mind."

"Roger." Mac typed frantically on the keyboard. She opened up a backdoor to the servers and linked them to Oversight's systems. Seconds later the data began to upload to the Oversight computers.

"We've got a connection. Once this is uploaded, we'll

wipe the data from their systems," Straub said. "I'm authorizing an immediate counter-mission. Destroy any samples you can of the virus."

"Roger that, Ice Pick. Legion: out." Mac switched back to her regular channel. She tapped the keyboard and started looking through the files. She found five active strands of Nestor. She'd have to destroy each. Mac holstered her pistol and grabbed her rifle. She paused before leaving the office and decided to check the desk. She smiled as she pulled out a bottle of rum. It was spiced rum with plenty of sugar. That played well for Mac's plans. She grabbed the bottle, a handful of paper towel and exited the room. She weaved through the labs until she stopped at a records room. She opened the door and peered inside. She saw stacks upon stacks of hard copies and samples. Each had played a part in the creation of the Nestor strands and each had to be destroyed. Mac jammed the paper towels into the bottle of rum. Seconds later she had a Molotov cocktail. She flicked Aeden Orman's zippo to life and lit the towel. With a sinister smile, Mac tossed the cocktail into the room. Seconds later the records room was burning brightly. Mac closed the door.

Mac weaved through the maze of labs as she made for the rear. Secure storage would be in the back. It was always in the back. She pushed open the door and quietly stepped in. She saw five tubes. Each went from the floor to the ceiling. Each tube had a small door that could only be opened by a secure nine-digit combination. Each tube had several wires running from the keypad to a different computer. Monitoring each of the computers was a WhiteStar soldier. Mac swiftly drew her silenced pistol and leveled it at the man. She squeezed of a single shot and put a bullet in the back of the man's skull. He crumpled to the ground.

Mac walked over to the first tube and examined it. Inside each tube were two things. One was a vial of blue liquid and the other was an emergency incinerator. The incinerator was a safety precaution. If something went wrong and there was a chance that the virus could escape then they would burn it. Better to start again then to have a massive loss of life, or worse. Mac glanced at the keypad. There was no way she could gain entry without the code. The dead soldier and his equipment had been trying to hack the keypad but with little success. Mac reached past the keypad, flipped opened the safety glass pressed hard on the first tube's incinerator button that lay underneath. A large tongue of bright flame filled the tube and engulfed the vial. Seconds later the vial and the first strand of virus was gone. Mac moved to the second and repeated the process, doing so for the third and forth as well. With each button pressed, the corresponding vial would vanish in a tongue of bright burning flame. Mac reached for the fifth and final button when she heard the sound of a weapon being cocked. Mac's hand recoiled and gripped her M4 tightly. She spun around and leveled the rifle at the door. She glared at the tall bald Russian that stood before her.

Morozko.

"Hello, little *Zaika*," he said with a smug. "I was hoping to see you again."

Mac arm echoed the pain it felt earlier. The memory of rolling off the cliff and falling hard to the ground flashed before her. Had that really been the same day? So much had happened since then. This day seemed endless. Mac forced her mind to focus. She forced her heartbeat to calm and her breathing to steady.

"Morozko," Mac growled. "Surrender now or you will die."

"Such brave words, *Zaika*," he said with a laugh. "I cannot surrender nor can you walk away. This is fact. We are two soldiers on either end of a battle. Our fight is inevitable."

"Is this where you give me a history lesson or a sob story?" Mac asked. "You Death Hounds never seem to shut up."

Morozko just laughed. He shook his head. "I have no sob story, Zaika. I am simply a mercenary working for the highest bidder. I have been one since my early days as a teenager. I have no sob story about the Evil British Empire or about my Abusive Father. I am simply one who fights for money to better support my family."

"What would they say if they knew what you were doing?" Mac asked.

"They know what I do. They know I fight in places and do things that are not kind but they also know that this world is not kind." The Russian was unwavering in his belief and his stance. "I do what I do for my wife and my daughter, my little *Kotyonok*."

"What if I could double your salary to come work for me?" Mac asked.

"I get paid a lot, Mac." It was the first time he'd used her name. Keane: they all knew her name because of him. "Doubling what I get paid would be an enormous amount."

"I wouldn't have made the offer if I couldn't cover it."

For a moment he looked tempted. She could see the dollar signs in his eyes. Morozko looked around the room and frowned. He shook his head. "I am a наемник. I have no morals but I still have honour. I cannot teach my daughter morals but I can teach her honour. I cannot accept."

"Shame," Mac said. "We could have used you."

"I was told I would be fighting Thantos," Morozko said. He lowered his PP-2000 and dropped it to the floor. "I wanted a good fight with him but I will not get it. Instead, I will fight you but not with guns but with our fist and skills and power, like God intended us to fight."

"I should just shoot you here," Mac threatened.

"You could try," he replied. "But I see that look in your eyes, *Zaika*. You are furious that you lost against me."

As much as she wanted to deny it, it was true. Mac didn't like losing; in fact she fucking hated it. This wasn't supposed to be some kids' show where the hero and the villain chatted first then decided on a fair fight but there they were, chatting like old friends.

"Shoot me, Mac," he taunted with a knowing smirk. "Shoot me and forever know that you *could not* best me."

Mac scowled as she unclipped her M4. She knelt down as she lowered the weapon to the floor. Mac didn't wait to get back up. She bolted from the crouched position and slid into a sweeping kick. Her speed was quick enough to catch Morozko's leg. The Russian's feet flew out from underneath him. Mac scrambled to her feet and bolted for the final incinerate button. She would worry about besting the Russian *after* she'd saved the world. A blast of ice caught her side and sent her flying across the room. She slammed into a wall, hard. Mac's lungs gasped for the air that had just been knocked from her.

"Naughty, naughty, *Zaika*." The Russian climbed to his feet. "Your focus should be on me, not the experiment."

"Do you know what that virus will do to the world?" Mac asked as she climbed to her feet.

"I do."

"Then let me destroy it."

"Honour says I cannot," Morozko said. "But if you best me, I will let you destroy it."

Mac scowled. This was *totally* some kids' TV show. Morozko backed from storage room and Mac reluctantly followed.

"I should warn you of two things," Mac cautioned. "The first is that I *never* lose twice,"

"And the second?"

"I am Thanatos' apprentice."

A hedonistic look crossed Morozko's face.

CHAPTER 16

Morozko's fists were fast. They came down from above and struck with the strength of a falling meteor. Mac did her best to dodge each blow. She knew that if these asteroids would to hit her, she would quickly become extinct. Mac stepped quickly, slapping aside the Russian's fist. She didn't want to block. Even with a block those fists could do damage.

Mac stepped forward with a speedy slip. She bobbed to the left as a thunderous punch passed where she once stood. Mac slipped into Morozko's left pocket and struck with a pair of body hooks. Each fist slammed into his side. Bit by bit she would chip away at this mountain until it came crashing down. Morozko twisted his waist and pivoted around. His right knee slammed against Mac and sent stumbling backward. He finished his spin and fired a kick. The powerful blow catching Mac in the chest and sent her flying backwards. She bounced off the floor twice before coming to a halt. Mac groaned. Every inch of pain she had suffered today was coming back. The cuts, the bruises and the arm; they all cried out at once. It was a reminder that she was mortal. It was a reminder that she was not a meta, she was simply human. It was also a reminder that she was still alive and as long as she was still breathing, she'd still be fighting.

"Come at me, *Zaika*," Morozko taunted at Mac climbed to her feet. "Show me your speed. Show me your wit. Show me your fire."

Mac walked forward with her hands held high with a fire in her eyes. Mac slipped into range, bobbing through his avalanche of punches. Mac stepped with her lead leg - her left - and leaned on it. Her right fist came out. It dropped first then came around in a looping motion. It was an overhand punch that came over her head and dropped down across his chin. Punching upwards was a battle against gravity. An overhand punch let gravity pull her fist down across Morozko's chin at 9.8 meters / second^2. As her right fist retracted her left shot out. It struck once into the Russian's side and once across his face. Morokzo stumbled back, surprised and stunned by her combo. He opened his mouth to speak but Mac never gave him the chance. She charged him. She leapt into the air, grabbed his head and used it to pull herself upward as she struck with a rising knee. The blow sent the Russian back even further. Mac landed back on her feet. She stood there with the same fire in her eyes but now she wore a smirk on her face. Gunner wasn't going to like it, she wasn't supposed to take pleasure in violence, but she was having fun. Mac was *really* enjoying this fight.

Major Renata Shatalov stood in the hostage room. She talked to Lt. Latif as a pair of Whitestar goons watched over the hostages. The door suddenly burst open as a third soldier stormed into the room. Shatalov's head spun around and eyed the soldier. He panted for several seconds before trying to speak.

"Fire!" He said between pants. "There is a fire on this floor. It's in the records room. All the hard copies are burning. Morozko is fighting the woman - Mac - right now."

Shatalov bolted out of the room. She stared at her tech-head on the computer. "Secure all digital copies, now."

"I...I can't," he said after several moments of typing. "It's being deleted. I'll save what I can but..." Shatalov already had left the room.

"She's wiping the project," Shatalov cursed. "It's all disappearing."

"Secure the room," Latif ordered. The soldiers nodded and moved to the doors. Shatalov moved towards Agent: Blindspot. She grabbed him by his jacket and pulled him away from the group. Gunner cried out in protest but Latif silenced him with a kick. Rath grumbled beneath his mask. Shatalov knelt before Blindspot and locked eyes with her hostage.

"It's all vanishing," she said with a calm demeanor. "Your project is vanishing in flames as we speak. Mac is destroying everything. She's burned the hard copies and she's wiping the files off of the servers. I can only expect that she is burning the live strains as we speak. The last ten years of your life will burn away and you will have accomplished *nothing*. Is that what you want?" Blindspot was wavering; both Shatalov and Gunner could see it. All he needed was one final push. "Tell me the code. Let me save your work. Let me save the last ten years of your life."

"Fine," Blindspot said. He began to recite the numbers.

"No!" Gunner cried out. He snapped his head around to Rath and cried out. "Now!"

Rath let out a roar as he called upon his super strength. With a single tug he snapped his bindings. He flipped to his feet and charged. Latif raised his rifle towards the masked man but never got a chance to fire off a round. Gunner hands - now free - grabbed the weapon and pointed it upwards. Gunner was free.

Gunner had an escape plan; he *always* had an escape plan. Hidden within his belt buckle was a small three-inch blade that could come out with a double-tap of the plate. When Rath roared, a terrifying distraction, Gunner used the blade to slice off his ziptie. He flipped to his feet and charged Latif. Gunner could have escaped at any time but he wasn't playing the role of soldier, he was playing bodyguard.

Gunner grabbed Latif's weapon. His left hand

grabbed the barrel and firmly pointed the barrel upwards. His right hand ejected Latif's mag and tossed it aside. Then he forced the trigger back. The rifle fired off its chambered round, emptying the weapon. Gunner grabbed Latif with both hands. With a pivot and turn, Gunner rolled the Canuck over his hip and slammed him down on the floor. Gunner tried to force his knee into Latif's neck but the Canadian was too quick. He kicked Gunner off of him and rolled to his feet. Guns were not a close range weapon. Gunner and Latif both knew this. So when Latif tossed aside the weapon, neither soldier was surprised. Latif withdrew his knife and shifted his stance. This had suddenly become a knife fight and Gunner was unarmed.

Three soldiers stared in terror as the roaring masked man charged at them. For a second they stood there, stunned. Who was this animalistic brute? Then, like a memory triggered by a smell, they suddenly remembered something: they had guns. The soldiers raised their rifles to fire. Rath had dealt with guns before. He was super strong but he wasn't invulnerable. Bullets still hurt the super-strong guy. Rath grabbed a table as he ran - a long metal table that normally took four people to move - and hoisted it into the air as a shield. Each bullet bounced off of the table with a metallic ding. Rath tossed the table and watched in glee as it collided with two soldiers. He swiftly pivoted and lashed for the third. He grabbed the soldier's rifle and snapped the barrel in one swift motion. The stunned soldier stared at his weapon is disbelief. Rath grabbed the man and tossed him across the room.

Rath's gaze quickly scanned the room. Shatalov was gone. He spotted an open door at the far end of the room. Rath bolted for it. As he exited the room he spotted four more soldiers in the hall. Each had their weapons pointed at the door and were waiting to shoot whomever emerged from it. The weapons cracked to life and Rath ducked back into the room.

Rath cursed. He hoped Mac was having better luck.

Mac was not having better luck. Any advantage she had gained early in the fight was quickly fading away. Mac struck with flurry after flurry of blows upon Morozko's body but it seemed to have no effect. Yet each blow he landed on Mac shattered her entire world. Each punch would resonate throughout her spine until every inch of her body hurt from it. Each kick would cause a shockwave of agony across her nervous system. The worst part was she was still enjoying herself. Mac couldn't remember the last time she had been challenged this much. She couldn't remember the last time her skills had been tested to this extreme.

Mac struck with another overhand punch. The fist came down across his chin. Only this time pain filled her hand. His chin had suddenly become as firm as a wall. She eyed him suspiciously and frowned as she saw a thin layer of blue ice forming around his skin. The fucker was using his ice powers to create a layer of armour.

"I am having fun, *Zaika*," Morozko said, "but it is time I stop playing around. I must end this fight now. My duties call to me."

Morozko raised his hand and a shard of ice appeared. In a flash he tossed it at her, like an icicle dagger. Mac dove to the side, the ice barely missing her. She looked up just in time to see a second one flying at her. It drove into her arm, into her left arm. Mac screamed. Morozko just smirked.

"What the fuck?" she asked between spasms of pain. "What the fuck is up with you and my left arm?"

Morozko eyed her quizzically. Had he forgotten that in their last battle he had dislocated her left shoulder? The only reason she escaped was by stabbing him in his left leg. Mac's eyes went wide. She'd forgotten that. She sighed. It had been a long day. Mac ripped out the icicle with a cry of pain.

Blood dripped down her body but she ignored it. She reached for her vest and withdrew her dagger. It was time to end this. Morozko eyed the weapon and formed a dagger of his own, albeit one made of ice.

"Is this the time for our final dance, *Zaika*?" He mocked.

"What the fuck does Zaika even mean?" Mac asked. "I need to know before I kill you."

The Russian just laughed. He charged Mac. His struck with his ice-dagger but Mac bobbed away. She slipped into his left pocket and tried to strike. Her knife sliced across his side but couldn't cut past his ice-armour. She swore again. The ice was thin but somehow it was incredibly thick and durable. She was really starting to hate the iceman and his unfair meta-powers. Morozko pivoted and swung, his fist covered once again in a glove of ice. Mac ducked beneath the blow and lashed out with a kick. Her foot slammed against the ice armour and sent pain up her leg and into her body. She *really* hated the armour.

Mac slipped to the left brought both arms up as another ice-fist dove for her. She couldn't dodge, she couldn't give up the position she had just gotten. Her arms both went numb as the ice-fist collided with her arms. Her arms felt heavy and she struggled to keep them up. Mac lashed with her foot. She wasn't going to make the same mistake as last time by striking the body, instead she went for his leg. She struck the exact spot on his leg where she had stabbed him earlier. It had seemed like days ago but it was only a few hours. Morozko didn't cry out in pain, he only winced. His leg buckled slightly but Mac didn't let up. She struck again, this time with her fist. It was a downwards punch into the wound. He grunted loudly but still he did not cry out. Mac grabbed her knife with both hands and stabbed deeply into the wound. Finally, Morozko cried out. It was a bloody-cry of agony as steel struck the same wounded flesh, muscles and nerve it had earlier. Morozko's leg finally gave way as the Russian fell to the ground. He tried to move, to scramble away but he couldn't. The pain was too great.

Morozko was beaten. Mac had won. She drew her M17 and leveled it at Morozko.

"I won," she panted.

Mac pulled the trigger.

Morozko didn't die. The bullet bounced off of his head. Mac swore. What the hell was it going to take to kill this guy? What was it going to take to get though his meta-ice armour? Mac looked across the room and saw a window. She paused for a second to get her bearings and smiled. The window was facing the perfect direction. She grabbed Morozko by his shirt and dragged him across the room. Each bump in his leg caused him greater pain.

"What does *Zaika* mean?" Mac asked as she dragged. Her curiosity had gotten the better of her.

"Your gun cannot kill me," Morozko said with an agony filled voice.

"Mine can't," Mac said as she reached the window. She hoisted Morozko up and slammed him against the window. In the distance she could see the armoury. Mac locked eyes with the Russian and spoke her final words to him. "But DJ's gun can."

"You may not be Thanatos but you are Death. She who trains under Death only does so to become Death. Mac, you are *Śmierć*: the female Grim Reaper. In Serbia they have a saying. It goes 'Death is not choosing a time, place or years'. It means that Death is destiny, it is your destiny."

"What does *Zaika* mean?" Mac repeated.

"*Zaika* means bunny. You are quick, you are clever and fast, like a bunny. I hope my daughter is like you," Morozko said. "Mac, my little Zaika."

DJ pulled the trigger.

Morozko was dead.

Gunner's body moved quickly as he tried to avoid Latif's knife. The Canuck's attacks were quick and accurate. It was, seemingly, only by luck and the grace of god that Gunner was still standing. Latif's skill with the blade was amazing. His fingers were nimble and he was deft with the steel. The knife would move or shift faster than Gunner could follow. But this wasn't the first time Gunner had faced a skilled knife user. Dealing with a knife user required three basic elements of combat: surprise, speed and violence of action.

The longer a knife fight went on, the more chance Gunner had at becoming a stuck pig. He couldn't stay on the defensive. He needed to shock Latif with his attacks. This was the surprise.

Switching from defense to offense in a knife fight, especially when one side didn't have a knife, had to be done swiftly. Any wasted seconds that occurred during the switch could be used against Gunner. This was the speed.

His attacks had to be an assault. There were no half-measures in a knife fight. Gunner couldn't simply strike Latif. A punch or a kick would do little to even the fight. It would just put Gunner at a position to get stabbed. He had to disable the attack and rid him of the knife. This was the violence of action.

Gunner dashed forward. His surprised attack forced Latif to stab him. Gunner's hands swiftly lashed out. They grabbed Latif's stabbing arm and locked around it. Ideally he could control the weapon arm and rid Latif of the weapon but the Canuck wasn't so easily taken. With a move that could only be done by someone who had spent hundreds of hours practising with the knife, Latif tossed the blade from his left hand to his unhindered right. Latif pivoted and slashed. Gunner released the left arm and lashed out at the right. Latif flung his knife again, this time in a flashy behind-the-back toss, and it landed back in his left hand. The knife slashed across Gunner's side but the soldier simply ignored it. He'd deal with the pain later.

Rath grabbed a chair and tossed it down the hallway. It flew like a fastball and did a massive amount of damage when it collided with a soldier. The sickening crunch brought a smile to Rath's mask-hidden face. He reached for another chair. Rath needed a way to get the hostages out and he was quickly running out of furniture. There were two doors and both were covered. There were a few walls he could punch through but he wasn't sure where in the building he was situated. The only directions remaining were up or down. Up was pointless; going higher wasn't going to free anyone. That left down. He'd have to smash a hole into the floor and lower the hostages to freedom. Rath looked across the room and saw Gunner and Latif fight. The knife wielder was good, scary good. Rath knew that Gunner could best Latif given enough time but they were in a hurry.

"Shake and bake!"

Gunner heard the cry and steadied himself. He wasn't sure *exactly* what Rath had planned but he knew it was about to get very uneven. Rath slammed his foot into the floor and the entire building shook. Latif, caught off-guard, stumbled and Gunner moved to meet him. He grabbed Latif's knife hand and twisted. Latif tossed the knife a third time but the throw was hasty and clumsy. Gunned snatched the knife out of the air as he twisted Latif's body to the ground. Gunner pinned Latif to the floor and pressed the knife against his throat. The floor shook again as Rath made a second and third kick. With the fourth and final kick, a hole formed in the ground.

"We have an exit," Rath yelled.

"Get them out of here!" Gunner yelled back.

One by one Rath started lowering the hostages to the floor below. He instructed each to run out of the building and find somewhere to hide. Gunner glanced back at the soldier pinned beneath him. "Why the Death Hounds?"

"It was for a secondary objective," Latif said. "Some guy named Thanatos killed Shatalov's father. She hoped to lure him out to kill him but he never showed."

"He was here the entire time. He was your hostage," Gunner chuckled. "I'm Thanatos." Gunner forced the knife into Latif's neck.

"You bastard!" Gunner grabbed the pistol from Latif's vest and rolled to the side. Gunner came to his feet. He saw Shatalov standing in the doorway with a vial in her hand and a P90 aimed at his head. "You're Thanatos? You killed my father? You are the reason we had to flee Russia. You're the reason my life was ruined."

Gunner's mind raced. Shatalov had him dead to rights. There was no way he could fire at her before she riddled him with bullets. He glanced at Rath but he could nothing. The only hostages remaining were Blindspot. Rath had told him to wait so they could better protect him. Now he was in danger, again.

"It's over!" Shatalov yelled as she walked in. She stood a few feet away from Gunner. She paused by the Rath's hole and glanced down. She saw all the hostages were gone but shrugged it off. She no longer cared. She had the virus and she had her father's killer. She scowled at Gunner. "You die today for the sins you've committed."

A gunshot rang out but not from Shatalov's P90. The bullet came from the second doorway and ripped through Shatalov's chest. Gunner glanced at the shooter and saw a bloodied and beaten Mac standing there, her M17 in her right hand as she used her M4 as crutch in her left. Mac squeezed the M17's trigger a second time and put a second round into Shatalov.

"Stay the fuck away from my father."

CHAPTER 17

This was a bad idea. Gunner knew it, Coriolanus knew it and even the social worker knew it. This was worse than bad, this was a terrible idea. So why was he here? Why were they going through all these motions if they all knew it was a bad idea? Why were they wasting everybody's time?

"This is a terrible idea," Gunner said, aloud this time. Coriolanus Redgrave ignored his apprentice. He just sat there and read a magazine.

"You excited for the Salt Lake Olympics?" Coriolanus said with mock interest. The 2002 games were several years in the past. Both Gunner and Coriolanus had participated in adjoining security missions for the event. "I wonder how we'll do in men's hockey."

The two men were sitting in the waiting lobby for an adoption agency. Expired magazines were scattered across the tables, minus the *extremely* out-of-date issue that Coriolanus currently read. Gunner was anxious and nervous. He was fidgeting in his seat.

"Hockey? What are you talking about?" Gunner asked, eyeing his mentor.

"Olympic ice hockey: it's a game you play it on ice with sticks and a puck." Coriolanus showed Gunner the magazine. The magazine had the iconic five rings on the cover and the words *How will we fare at home?* on the cover. "Do you think we'll do better than Nagano?"

"I need you to be serious," Gunner said.

"I hope we cream the Czechs this time around," Coriolanus said, ignoring his apprentice's pleas. "Maybe we'll even place." Gunner sighed. There would be no talking to his mentor in this state.

"The US win a medal in hockey? Psshh. We'll get our asses handed to us by the Canucks," Gunner said, finally playing along. "Besides, it's the *Winter Olympics*. Nobody cares. It's summer or nothing."

"I've trained you so well but after comments like that I wonder if you learned anything at all," Coriolanus said with a sigh. He lowered the magazine and stared at Gunner. "What's wrong, Kid?"

"How many years do I have to work for you before I stop being *Kid*?"

"When you stop *acting* like one." Gunner rolled his eyes and looked away. He nervously eyed the door as sweat rolled down his balding dome. Coriolanus dropped the magazine on the table. He knew what the problem was. "If this was a mistake, we wouldn't have gotten this far. If the adoption agency didn't think you'd be a good fit they wouldn't have let us get to this stage."

"I know that it's just..." Gunner's words trailed off. Coriolanus leaned back in his chair. He was an older man, coming on retirement faster than he was comfortable with. He was a man filled with questions of his own. What did a man with a head full of secrets and bad memories - neither of which he wanted - do with retirement? Somehow golf didn't seem to cut it. But his questions were for another day. Gunner's questions were the topic of the hour.

"Clara, Laura and Sondra," Gunner listed. "I couldn't look after them and they were adults. How am I supposed to look after *her*?" Gunner pointed to the large metal door. "People die around me, Cori. I can't put that on her. She's an innocent and she's so young."

"I know you're afraid to grieve again," Coriolanus explained. "But this is different. This isn't grieving; this is you healing and moving on. This is you becoming the best you possible. This is growth. This is you *finally* growing the fuck up."

"You can't say that to a man who's losing his hair," Gunner snapped.

"You've been losing hair since pre-school, Charlie Brown," Coriolanus laughed. The sound of an opening door caught both of their attention. Both men sprung to their feet as a social worker emerged. Coriolanus clamped his hand on Gunner's shoulder. He looked his apprentice in the eyes and gave him a reassuring smile. "Just go in there and meet her. If things don't work out, then they don't. But you can't go saying that you'll shoot yourself in the foot when you haven't even loaded the gun."

"One time," Gunner protested. "I shot myself in the foot one time and you've never let me forget it."

"Well I've *never* shot myself in the foot."

"And I didn't shoot myself in the foot," Gunner continued. "I shot a man who suddenly developed metal skin and the bullet ricochet off of his skin and dove into my foot." Gunner froze. He turned around and smiled at the social worker. She was giving the pair a confused look. Gunner quickly lied. "It was a video game. Dude loves his video games. He's like 'when can we play more video games' and I have to be like 'not today, Old Man, not today'. He loves his video games...."

"This is you *finally* growing the fuck up," Coriolanus repeated with a shake of his head.

The woman shrugged as she escorted Gunner into another room. There was a large brown couch. Sitting on one side was a small girl with long raven-coloured hair. Gunner sat down on the other side of the couch. The two sat in silence, each stealing glances at each other.

"I'm not looking for a father," the girl quickly snapped in a tough and defensive tone.

"I'm not looking for a daughter," Gunner quickly retorted.

Silence.

"Are you a weirdo?" the girl asked.

"A little bit, how about you?" Gunner asked.

"A little bit," the girl sheepishly replied.

Silence.

"Can you cook?" Gunner asked.

"No," she hesitantly replied.

"Damn, neither can I," Gunner said in a joking manner. "You and I may be in trouble then, Kiddo."

The girl looked at Gunner for a long moment before a reluctant smile crept out across her lips. Gunner's lips did the same. He reached across the couch and offered the girl his hand. "I'm Gunner."

She stared at it for a few moments before taking it. The two shook. "I'm Bailee."

Major Renata Shatalov's body went limp. She dropped to her knees before losing all strength and falling down through the hole in the floor. She fell down to the floor below and collided with a sickening thud but nobody paid her any attention. Everybody was focused on Mac.

Gunner scrambled to his feet and bolted across the room. He dove into a feet-first slide as Mac began to fall. He caught her in his arms before she hit the floor. For a moment Gunner did nothing save for holding Mac and in turn Mac did nothing save enjoy the comfort that Gunner's strong arms provided.

"You're late, Kiddo," Gunner quietly said.

"Sorry, Old Man, but traffic was fucking terrible," she muttered back.

"You okay, boss lady?" Rath asked.

Mac winced as she sat up. She smiled at her teammate and nodded. "It's better than it looks."

"It pretty much fucking has to be," Rath said. "What the hell happened to you?"

"I've just been running around in the forest," Mac

said. "I always forget, that's more your thing." Rath growled. Mac just smiled.

"What's our status?" Gunner asked.

"Zapper, Speedy and the Iceman are all dead," Mac said as Rath handed her some water. Mac took several gulps before speaking once more. "The hostages control the dorms and DJ is on overwatch with a long gun in his hands."

"He must be happy," Rath snickered.

"Zetes is on secondary channels giving me support and Keane is a fucking traitor."

"Wait, what?"

"What about the virus strands?" Blindspot demanded. Mac eyed the man with an angry glare.

"I burned the records, wiped the servers and destroyed four strands. I think she had the fifth."

"Why? Who gave you that permission?"

"They were breaching our system. Destroying it before they got a hold of it seemed like a better option."

Gunner reached into Mac's backpack and withdrew her first aid kit. He quickly pried it opened and began to examine the wounds. He started with the shoulder wound.

"What now?" Rath asked.

"We get the rest of the soldiers, retake the base and then get a beer? Rath's buying." Gunner smirked. "I'm in the mood for some *really* expensive beer."

"Shatalov's on the move." DJ's voice came through her radio. Mac's body was tired and exhausted but the sniper's word cut right through the fatigue. Her body tensed up.

"Say again, DJ."

"Shatalov is moving. I....shit." The line went quiet for several seconds. "She's firing at me. Shatalav is moving towards the vehicle bay."

"How the fuck?" Mac pushed Gunner away and scrambled to the hole in the floor. She stared down it and, surprisingly, she saw no body laying there. She only saw an empty vial. "Shit, shit, shitting shit!"

"How the fuck did she survive two shots to the gut?"

Rath asked.

"The vial," Blindspot said with a triumphant laugh. "She took the damn vial. She injected the Nestor virus strain *into* herself. The virus is healing her."

"DJ," Mac ordered across the radio. "Take her out. She cannot be allowed to escape."

"I don't have a shot," DJ radioed back. "She's escaping on a motorcycle."

"Shit, shit, shitting shit!" Mac repeated, louder this time. "DJ: pull back and meet us at the vehicle bay. We're going to follow her."

"Confirm."

"*Trautman*, come in." Gunner opened his mouth to protest but Mac silenced her with a raised finger.

"This is *Trautman* Actual."

"Do we have any drones in the area?"

"Negative, Raven," Grammer Ford replied. "They are on route but won't be in range for a couple hours."

"Shit. Keep eyes on Shatalov. We cannot let her escape." Mac turned to Gunner and Rath. "Grab a gun and some ammo. We're going after her."

"You can't, Kiddo," Gunner protested. "You're a wreck. Let me finish this for you."

"I'm not done until this is," Mac growled. "You taught me that."

"I also taught you that a man's gotta know his limitations."

"No you didn't, that was from *Magnum Force*."

"Close enough. I mean I am basically Clint Eastwood," Gunner said with a shrug. He eyed Mac with worried eyes. She narrowed hers and stared back. Gunner sighed. He walked to the nearest fallen soldier and stole himself a rifle. He pocketed some ammo and cocked the weapon. "Let's get this over with then."

The trio exited the building as DJ steered a large pickup towards them. Mac moved for the driver's seat but stumbled slightly. She winced as she caught herself. Her arm hurt, her chest hurt and her head hurt. She was in no position to be driving.

"Rath," Mac said quickly as she approached the truck. "You've got the wheel, Gunner's on shotgun and DJ on overwatch."

"I'll take the back, Kiddo. You take shotgun." Mac opened her mouth to object but thought better of it. She climbed into the truck's cab.

"*Trautman*, come in." Mac drew her M17 and removed the silencer.

"This is *Trautman* Actual."

"Do you have her?"

"Yes we do, Raven," Grammer Ford said. "She's heading towards Port Alexander."

"That has a seaplane base," Gunner said. "She can't be allowed to take off."

"*Trautman*, Shatalov cannot be allowed to take off. This is an Alpha Threat quarantine issue. Ground all flights, professional and private, and make sure no boats or ships leave either."

"Roger that, Raven."

Mac looked back at her team. "She's got a head start. Load up and let's move."

"Is she always this bossy with you guys?" Gunner asked. Rath and DJ glanced at each other.

"I ain't saying shit while she's right there," DJ said quickly. All three men laughed. Mac rolled her eyes but couldn't help but let a smirk slip through. Gunner climbed into the back of the truck and glanced at the box full of ordinates. He let out a low whistle as he dragged his fingers across the grenade launcher. "I decided to raid the armoury, just in case." Gunner raised a quizzical eyebrow.

"Just in case," DJ repeated with a smile.

The truck slowed at the edge of the base. At the point where the base became the forest, along one of only two roads out, the truck came to a halt. A large tree had fallen across the road, purposely cut as such to prevent any vehicles from entering or exiting the base. Mac had passed that log hours earlier on her attempt to enter the base. Had that only been six hours ago? It felt like days.

Mac exited the truck, her rifle up and ready. She eyed the log. It was exactly like before only this time there was a makeshift ramp leaned up against it. The ramp wouldn't hold a truck or a car but for a motorcycle it would do perfectly. Shatalov used the ramp to jump the log like some twelve-year old boy on a bike.

"It'll take me a couple minutes to move this," Rath said.

Mac nodded. She held her M4 up as she scanned the surrounding woods. If the ramp was a lie, if it was bait to lure them to a halt, then this point would be a perfect ambush. She glanced to her left and saw Gunner doing the exact same thing. Mentor and student - father and daughter - scanned for an ambush.

"I got nothing," Gunner called out.

"I don't hear anything," DJ said. His voice wavered a little. "I don't hear *anything*, at all."

Mac frowned. She could taste the forest air but felt no wind on her skin. No sound emanated from the trees. Tongass National Forest was full of plants and animals. It was a hive of life and noise. That much life was never silent. Mac glanced up in the air and saw a bald eagle flying above. It wasn't passing by, it was simply circling above. It made Mac uneasy.

She pulled M4's sling off of her body and dumped the weapon in the back of the truck. She reached into DJ box of stolen goodies and removed two smoke grenade, a flash bang and four grenades. She pocketed each.

"I'll be right back," Mac said.

"Kiddo?" Gunner asked.

"I'll be okay, Old Man. I just have to take care of something."

The eagle stopped circling and flew inwards, deeper into the forest. Mac followed it. Shatalov's Death Hounds were made up Morozko, Taranis, Ultraviolet and Dryad. The popsicle, the socket and the roadrunner were all dead. That simply left one person.

Mac walked into a small clearing of trees and glanced up. High atop a tree, perched on a branch it had no business being on, was the blade eagle. With its distinctive eyes it glared down at her like some American deity judging her patriotism. A sound caught her attention and Mac turned to her left, drawing her pistol as she did. She leveled her weapon at the sound and found her sights lined up on a familiar female grizzly.

"Hello, girl," Mac whispered. She pivoted to her right and saw three Archipelago wolves, each with dark grey fur, slowly approaching. She frowned and slowly holstered the weapon. "Good boy."

It would be rare for two of these beasts, majestic as they were, would be in the same area together. It would be impossible for all three. Any suspicions she had was now verified. Mac reached into her bag and withdrew two smoke grenades. She popped the pin on each and tossed one a few paces to her left and the second a few paces to her right. Each canister ignited and emitted a large billowing pillar of purple smoke. The two pillars of purple smoke grew in size and they echoed upwards. The bear remained still as it eyed the smoke. The wolves did the same. Each creature looked as if it was struggling to make a decision. Each animal was being urged to lunge or attack but their instincts were fighting against it. The bear was the first to crack. It turned away and walked off. Mac walked further into the clearing, drawing the flash bang from her bag as she did. She popped the pin and pitched the grenade behind her. Mac closed her eyes and covered her ears as it detonated. When Mac opened her eyes she glanced to her right. The wolves were gone. She looked up. Only the bald eagle remained.

"A long time ago," Mac began, speaking loudly. "A man took a city girl and moved her to the country. The city girl *hated* it. Nature was so stupid and icky and smelly. Worse of all, no matter what she did to try to manage nature it never worked. The city girl turned to the man and asked why? Do you know what he told her? He told her that you can never control nature. It is a living ball of chaos. That day the city girl learned that the only way to be one with nature was not to try and control it but to respect it instead.

"You convinced those animals to attack me but you forgot about their instinct. When animals see smoke, even purple smoke, their instinct tells them to run and flee. To an animal smoke means fire and fire means danger. Add in a loud and sudden noise and even the strongest of packs will turn tail and run. It's not their fault; it's just their survival instinct."

"You killed my brother," a voice yelled from the trees. "You put a bullet in his head and killed him."

Mac watched as Einin Moran emerged from the trees. Einin had a pistol in her hand and had it aimed at directly at her. Mac quickly drew a frag grenade. She popped the pin but held the trigger firmly. She eyed Dryad as she approached.

"My brother was a good man. He fought for what was right in this world. He fought against an oppressive government. He did some bad, we both have, but it was always to fight the good fight," Einin roared. "He didn't deserve to die, not like a fucking dog."

"You both knew the risks when you accepted this mission," Mac said calmly. "He played and he lost. That's how the game works."

"Our life and our fight are not a *fucking* game!" Einin was furious. "Now you die like he did."

Einin began to squeeze the trigger but Mac was faster. Mac lobbed the grenade and instead of firing Dryad dove to the side. The grenade exploded but nobody was harmed. Dryad spun to her feet and scanned the field. Mac was nowhere to be seen. Dryad screamed in anger and squeezed off three rounds, each in a random direction. She wanted to fight Mac, she wanted to kill her but the woman was fast and she was quiet. Dryad reached out with her powers as she tried to find the soldier but she was nowhere to be found. Mac was only visible when Mac *wanted* to be visible.

The fight didn't last long. Mac emerged from the shadows and struck. Her hands were quick. She grabbed Dryad, ripped the gun from her hand and tossed the woman to the ground. Einin scrambled to her feet and tried to strike back but she was no match for Mac. Unlike Orman and Morozko, Einin wasn't a skilled fighter. Mac struck the woman thrice before pitching her back to the ground.

"I killed your brother," Mac began. "I killed a great many people today and still have a few more to go. I don't want to add you to that list so I'm going to give you an offer. Walk away."

"You killed my brother," Einin stuttered. "I can't let this go."

"I know, I couldn't either in your shoes, but let's be honest. You're not killing me today. You can't fight worth a damn and you don't know shit about your powers. Do yourself a favour and walk away. Live to fight another day. Go train, get better and if you still feel raw about what happened here today," Mac said, "then come find me. I'll be waiting."

Mac drew her M17 and leveled it at the woman. Einin stared up in silence. Neither woman moved; they just locked eyes. Einin raised both hands in the air and slowly climbed to her feet. She back away and kept moving until she vanished in the trees. Mac lowered her weapon. She glanced upwards. The eagle was gone.

CHAPTER 18

Port Alexander wasn't a city; it wasn't a town or even a village. Port Alexander wasn't big enough to be any of those. With a population of 54 Port Alexander was *at best* a hamlet. It was located to the south of Baranof Island. There were few, if any, official roads traveling the distance. The few that existed were ill kept, dangerous dirt roads. Driving them required low speeds and full concentration. The truck violently bounced and everybody inside bounced with it. It took two hours to reach the hamlet.

Port Alexander used to be the salmon capital of the world. It used to have a population of 2500 but that was nearly a century ago. Now it was little more than the fading echo of a time past. The hamlet had dozens of buildings, most of which went unused. When Rath steered the truck into the hamlet, the other three quickly readied themselves.

"What do you hear?" Mac asked.

DJ tilted his head. "I don't know. It's weird. I'm only hearing one heartbeat but it's too loud. It's like it's echoing across the town."

"There is only one person?" Gunner asked.

"I...I don't know. This is new, even for me," DJ winced.

"Keep your eyes open and your gun ready," Mac said as she exited the truck. She grabbed her rifle and did a quick weapons check. "Everybody on me."

The filed through the town with their weapons raised. Rath carried only a pistol; the muscle never needed much more. DJ reluctantly ditched the long gun for a rifle. With each step inward DJ's face began to show more and more discomfort. Gunner glanced at the sniper. "You okay?"

"I can't focus. This echo is killing me. It's like thoughts are bouncing around in my head like a squash ball." DJ shook his head. "I can't even pick up nearby sounds. Someone could sneak up on me and I wouldn't even notice it until they were right above me."

"We're a team," Rath said from beneath his mask. "You just keep your eyes peeled and leave the hearing to us."

"How about we leave the hearing to guy who isn't covering his ears with a mask," DJ suggested. Gunner snickered. Mac fought a smile but one emerged anyways. Gunner was use to running solo but that wasn't Mac forte. Things were always better when she had a team, when she had her team.

A noise came from down the street and Mac and Gunner's weapons snapped up in that direction. A pair of men stumbled forward. Their footsteps were clumsy, like a baby horse taking their first steps, but seeing how each carried a weapon, their intent was obvious. As they stumbled closer, and the team got a better look at the two men, their eyes went wide and the jaw fell open. The two men were obviously fishermen. They had cracked skin and tired bodies but what really brought alarm was the colour of their skin: bright blue.

"What the actual fuck?" DJ asked.

"The Nestor Virus," Gunner spat. "It works. Shatalov is controlling them; they are part of her hive mind."

"Welcome to my hive," the two men said. They spoke as one, in perfect timing. Despite the words coming from each of their mouths, they weren't speaking their own words. The accent and the tone, it was Shatalov speaking. "There is so much to learn about being a hive mind but it feels so good. I know everything these people know and they each know everything I know. Admittedly that means they suddenly know how to soldier whereas I suddenly know way too much about fishing, but I'm just getting started. Imagine how much better I'll be when I absorb all of you."

"That's not happening," Mac growled. The two blue men raised their hunting rifles and aimed them directly at Gunner. "Surrender now, Shatalov, before more innocents die."

"I am no longer Shatalov," she said. "I am now Legion, for we are m---"

Mac and Gunner each fired a single shot. Each bullet dropped one of the blue-men, interrupting their speech. Mac whispered. "The name's taken. Find another."

Shatalov paced back and forth. She was in the lobby of the Port Alexander Seaplane Base. All flights were grounded and ships were allowed to leave. She was stuck in this nothing place. She needed a way out. Two twinges of pain shot through her body. Two of her drones were dead. She closed her eyes and tried to focus. She could feel each and every one of her drones. She saw what they saw, knew what they knew and could now do what they did. Their hearts even beat as hers did. The downside was she also felt what they felt. If one felt pain, she felt it and Mac and Gunner were killing her drones.

It had taken her almost no time at all to spread the virus. Within the two hours she had infect nearly the entire population - small as it was - of Port Alexander. Now all she had to do was learn how to control them. It was difficult. She was controlling them all, completely. She made them walk, she made them talk and she made them fight. None of which were easy. Her drones didn't have minds of their own, she'd accidentally overwritten them with her desires. With time, she would control them better. With practise she could infect someone without destroying their minds but until then she had to make do with what she had.

Pain.

Three more drones had just died. She had tried to rely on her military training, on the actions and decisions that were instinct for her by now. Her drones were moving better now but they were still using skills they had never encountered before. It was like taking a theory and putting it into practise. But still, the benefits were amazing. Shatalov glanced at her hand. The blue skin was disconcerting. It would make it impossible to hide but perhaps, with time and practise, she could return it to normal. With practise she could become something divine.

Mac released the trigger and ducked back behind the cover the building wall provided. She ejected one mag and reloaded another. Beside her Gunner kept a steady stream of bullets firing from his rifle. The blue-men were still stumbling about but their movement had become more militaristic. They were moving like Mac would, they were moving like soldiers. They were lining up in formation, using covering fire on moves and even circling around in an attempt to flank them. Their movements and formations were sloppy, and their weapons were limited to shotguns, pistols and hunting rifles, but they were getting better with each passing second.

Mac and her team were pushing towards the Seaplane Base but Shatalov was putting as many blue-men between them as possible. They had her team pinned. Mac looked at the building they were using for cover. It was a redbrick building that had to be almost a hundred years old.

"We need a hole."

"Really?" Rath said as he eyed the building. He frowned. "Do we have any other option?"

"Seriously, now?" Mac snapped. "What is your thing for old houses?"

"Fine," Rath said with a grumble. He slammed through the wall and into the building, cringing as he did. Rath adored old houses. They were buildings that stood the test of time. They were buildings that had faced down history and were still standing. Not many could do that.

"Get in!" DJ ducked into the building and Gunner followed. Mac was the last one in. The moment she stepped in Rath pushed a large oak bookshelf before the hole. Then he quickly put a couch before that. He then paused and studied the wall. He sighed in relief. His hole hadn't caused much in the way of structural damage.

"We need a plan," Mac panted. She moved to the nearest window and peered out. The blue men were still approaching. She looked in the distance and pointed to the airport. "Port Alexander Seaplane Base: I'm putting money that Shatalov is there."

"The question is how do we get there?" Gunner asked. He glanced at the grenade launcher strapped to Rath's back. "What if we pushed them back? If they are connected then maybe we can trigger Shatalov's instincts."

"She's a soldier," DJ added. "A firefight is common place for her but if we start blowing shit up then she'll flee."

"Cause all soldiers run away when things start exploding," Mac finished. She eyed her team. "Okay, all *normal* soldiers." The group chuckled. "Okay, Gunner. Light it up. Everybody else, pop and throw."

Explosions ripped through the town and Shatalov flinched at each one. All across Port Alexander her hive began to flee. They were ducking for cover and retreating back to somewhere safe. Her hive was retreating back to her. Shatalov screamed in anger. She grabbed the nearest chair, the only thing not bolted down in the airport, and whipped it against the wall. It was fucking infuriating. She had them cornered, the slayer of her team and the killer of her father, but now they had escape. She was a victim to her emotions and instincts. What she felt, she felt fifty times over. She felt fear for each man, woman and child she had absorbed and she felt it all at once. It was overwhelming. She had to regroup, she had focus. She was no some green soldier, still wet behind the ears. She was Major Renata Shatalov. She was ex-French Foreign Legion and she was the leader of the Смертельные Гончие. She was more than just a Death Hound. She was the *Alpha* Death Hound. She would not be stop by Death and Death's Daughter.

Shatalov closed her eyes and focuses. She reached out to her hive - no. It was a hive no longer. Hounds didn't have hives, they had packs. Shatalov reached out to her pack and tightly gripped each. Her favourable position was lost and she couldn't get it back. She could prepare an ambush. Mac was obsessive, much like her, and the Visegar bitch would pursue her endlessly. Shatalov could use Mac's obsessions to her advantage. She pulled her pack to the seaplane base. One by one, as the pack entered, Shatalov ordered them to a window or a ledge. Mac was coming and Shatalov would be ready.

Gunner pouted as the grenade launcher ran dry. The Old Man had been having *way* too much fun with the weapon. No normal man should enjoy blowing stuff up *that* much. But then again, Gunner was far from a normal man. Mac kept her rifle up as she crept forward. The blue men had retreated, as hoped. The question was where had they retreated to?

"They're in the seaplane base," DJ said, a relieved tone in his voice. "The endless echo is gone, kind of."

"The villagers are free?" Rath asked. DJ shook his head.

"No, but they aren't all around us," DJ explained. "I

used to hear the *exact* same heartbeat coming from all directions when they had us surrounded. It created a mind-numbing echo. Now I hear that same heartbeat, highly amplified, coming from one direction. It's like a beacon we're supposed to follow."

"Like the infamous four knocks," Rath said. The others eyed him. "Shut up, I watch TV."

"Well if she is inviting us forward," Mac said, "then I'm not one to disappoint."

"*Trautman* this is Jackal," Gunner said over a stolen radio. He used his common code name. "Do we have air support?"

"Armed drones are on route," a stunned Grammer Ford said on the other end. "They should be over your position in 45 seconds."

"Target the Seaplane Base," Gunner ordered. "And fire. You have my authorization."

"What are you doing?" Mac snapped. "There are innocents there. We have to see if we can free them."

"We have to contain this, Mac. We cannot let this virus out." Gunner frowned. Mac knew it was true but it still hurt. She was supposed to be the hero, not the killer. "I'm ordering this so you don't have to, so none of you have to."

"Base in range, Jackal," a voice came across the radio. "Confirm fire?"

"Orders confirmed. Fire at will."

Then the base exploded.

Shatlov checked the boat's engine when she heard the blast. At the same moment she dropped to one knee, her body screaming in pain. Then, as quick as the pain came, it vanished. It was like her entire pack had cried out at once and then was suddenly silenced. She forced herself to her feet and walked to the steering wheel. She turned the key and smiled as the engine turned over and roared to life. The boat was a high-power speed boat. She would speed off and be in Port Protection in a couple hours. Then she'd sneak into British Columbia, Canada, and vanish. It wouldn't matter where she was. With the Nestor, and enough time to get stronger with it, she'd be unstoppable. Shatalov stared at her hand. She focused her attention on the virus and willed it inwards. The blue skin receded inwards until she looked normal once more. She hoped Nestor would heal her innards like it had earlier. Shatalov walked to the dock and began to untie the line.

"You almost had me" a voice said suddenly. Shatalov looked over and spotted Mac standing on the dock, slowly approaching from Shatalov's left side. "When the Seaplane Base exploded I thought it was over. I thought you were dead. But as I watched it burn there was this nagging thought in my head. Why would she make herself into such a big target? Any Major worth their salt, especially one in Special Forces, would know we would have just blown up the damn building. So why hide there?"

Shatalov glanced back at the boat. Her P90 rested on a chair. That only left the Glock 17 on her right hip. She glanced back at Mac. The woman had a M4 hanging around her neck. It wasn't raised or even properly gripped. It was just hanging there. Shatalov's right hand slowly slid away from the rope and crept to her holster.

"Then I remembered what you and I have in common, Renata. We're survivors," Mac continued. "You put all of your blue men in that building and got them to shoot loudly and shoot a lot. You made them the biggest target you could while you snuck out the back. I wouldn't exactly call it honourable but those who run away live to fight another day."

"Is that what we do, Mac, we fight now?" Shatalov asked as her fingers reached the holster. "Do you and I soldier this out with fists and guns?"

"I rather not," Mac said. "After the shit you and yours put me through today, I don't know if I could survive a fight with you. I do know, however, that you sure as hell won't.

So why don't you just surrender and let's call this a day. You played the game and you lost but damn if you didn't play well."

Unlike Einin, Shatlov smiled. That was their life in a nutshell. They were stuck in a game that never-ended. One side stole a McGuffin and then the other side stole it back, repeat as necessary. Still in her kneeling position, the Major glanced at Mac. "You, more than anybody, know that the game never ends. I may have lost this round but you never stop playing, not in our lifestyle."

"There is one way out," Mac reminded. "Don't make me choose it for you."

"I'll see you in the next round, Mac," Shatalov said. "It's always nice to have a good player to compete against."

Shatalov's right hand moved like a blur. She pulled the Glock free of its holster and twisted her torso so to aim it at Mac but the younger woman was too fast. Mac's hand pulled the M17 free and squeezed of two rounds. Each tore a hole through Shatalov. Her body dropped to the surface of the wooden dock. Mac quickly approached. She kicked the Glock into the water and rolled Shatalov onto her back.

"Bailee MacIntosh," Shatalov said with pain gasps. "Death looks good on her." Mac lined her pistol up with Shatalov's forehead. The Major smiled and, with two fingers, tipped an imaginary hat. "Until the next game."

Mac pulled the trigger.

Major Renata Shatalov was dead.

Mac dropped to one knee, exhaustion once again taking a hold of her body and this time it wasn't letting go. Mac stared at the Major's body and the pool of cobalt blood that was forming beneath it.

It was finally over.

CHAPTER 19

Mac had been in firefights and she had been in car crashes. She had survived an explosion, she'd jumped from a burning plane, she'd been shot and more than once, and had to escape from a third world prison. Each of those instances was bad but she would willingly repeat them all over paperwork and debriefings. Nothing took the cool out of a spy mission like the bureaucratic touch. It had been nearly twenty-three hours since the end of the mission and she had yet to sleep or go home. All she had done was talk and listen and listen and listen. Everybody had their own thoughts on the mission and how it could have gone differently. Did she have to do this? Could she have done that instead? How could have this all been avoided? Mac hated it all.

Gunner and Rath stayed behind to watch over the containment procedures. Nobody wanted the Nestor - assuming there was still some remaining - to get out. Mac felt better knowing that Gunner and his Legion touch were supervising. She wanted to do it herself but nobody was going to allow that.

Mac had hoped that a debrief would at least answer some unresolved questions, like who recruited Keane and how he found out about Project: Nestor, but instead it left her with more questions. It turned out Keane was speaking the truth. He knew *nothing* about Project: Nestor. He didn't even release the location of Morrell Blood. His contact already had that information.

How did WhiteStar learn of Morrell Blood and Nestor?

Mac also wanted to know what Blindspot's plan was with Nestor but she knew that was never going to get answered. Senior management didn't report to operators like her. Every time she asked the question the topic got quickly changed to a flurry of thanks from the big brass. Everybody was thankful to her but nobody wanted to tell her anything. It was infuriating and tiring so Mac did what spies do best: she vanished. She waited for a quiet moment before ducking out and heading home.

Mac entered her townhouse from the garage and stumbled across the floor. She kicked off her boots and walked to the fridge. She pulled it open and swore. She was out of beer. Fuck. She was supposed to go buy some on her way home from lunch at the damned cafe. Mac rolled her eyes and stumbled into the living room. She plopped down on the couch and lay back. She was done trying to get to know the world that she saved so often, at least for today. She just wanted to lie back and be alone.

"Why is there *another* motorcycle in our garage?" A stern voice cried out. Mac sighed. It was hard to be alone when she had a roommate. "You get the shit kicked out of you on a regular basis *without* being on a bike. What happens when you have an accident *on* a bike?"

"I've already been in a motorcycle accident before," Mac told her roommate, Holly Silverburgh. "This was two years ago in Rome. I was chasing down some gunrunner when---"

"Shut up," Holly snapped. "That's not the point. You don't need another bike." Holly spoke of Shatalov's 1995

Ducati Super Sport 600 Scrambler that now belonged to Mac. It was a gift from Gunner.

"I didn't need my first bike either," Mac defended. "I *wanted* one. Just like I never *needed* a roommate to afford this place..."

"Liar," Holly laughed. "You definitely need me. I'm your best friend and your doctor." After high school Holly went to Med School. She became a doctor and was hired by Croxallé, a medical company owned by Visegar.

"You are my best friend who happens to be a doctor. You're not *my* doctor."

"Bullshit," Holly said as she plopped down next to Mac. "I've stitched you up more than anybody else."

"I never should have gotten you that job with Crox-allé," Mac teased.

"You bitch!" Holly said with a smack on Mac's shoulder. Mac winced but Holly didn't regret her decision. "All you did was drop my name. I was the one who aced my interview. I was the one who had the grades to impress them. I was the one who worked my ass off to rise through the ranks in that place."

When Holly got a job at Croxallé Mac suggested they buy a house together. Mac wanted someone she could talk to about her spy life and nobody was better than her BFF who now worked for the same company.

"What are you doing here any ways?" Mac asked. "Aren't you supposed to be spending the night at Roxy's place?"

"Meh, she's getting needy. Why are women so needy?" Holly joked. Roxy was Holly's latest girlfriend. The doctor seemed to go through women faster than tissues.

"Don't ask me, you're the lesbian. Needy women are totally your thing."

"I guess I'm attracted to what annoys me."

"It explains the time you kissed me," Mac joked. Holly smacked her again. The two friends just smiled at each other.

"Dr. Hammett called me and let me know what you went through. I decided to cancel and spend the night here instead."

"And you didn't bring beer?" Mac made tsk tsk noises.

"I had to check up on you. I am your doctor after all," Holly said. "Besides, I know what meds you're on. There is *no* way you should be drinking."

Mac opened her mouth to protest but a knock at the door interrupt them both. "That better be beer," Mac said as she climbed to her feet and answered it.

"I've got beer," Gunner said as Mac opened the door.

Mac smiled at the Old Man and grabbed a beer before inviting him in. He smiled at Holly and offered her a beer. Holly tried to protest but decided against it. With an exasperated sigh and an overly dramatic toss of her hands Holly gave up fighting and accepted the beer.

"Thanks for the bike," Mac said.

"You're the one I have blame for that?" Holly said. "You're not helping out at all."

"I'm supposed to be helping? That's news to me," he laughed. "How's our girl?"

"Broken, bruised and bitchy," Holly laughed. "Which is basically her normal state."

"Good," Gunner said. The three sat on the couch. "So what do y'all wanna do? We watch a movie or something?"

Ma and Holly glanced at each other and a sinister smile crossed their lips. Gunner's eyes went wide with terror and he rapidly shook his head.

Mac spoke first. "Let's watch *Wild Things*."

"Not again," Gunner groaned. "Do you girls even take that out of your DVD player?"

"Blueray or nothing, Mr. Powell," Holly explained. "We need that cheesiness in HD."

Mac took a swig of her beer and smiled. The rest of the world be damned. This was what she fought for, over and over. Beer, friends and infinite re-watches of *Wild Things*. The opening credits rolled across the screen but Mac never saw them.

She was already asleep.

EPILOGUE

Dr. Joni Polito stared at her apartment. It was cold and unused; since taking on Project: Nestor she hadn't lived in the apartment. It was cold and dusty but it would have to be her base of operations for the future. She walked to her TV and turned it on. It blinked to life with a blue screen. She walked to her movie shelf, withdrew a copy of *Battle Beyond the Stars* and inserted it into the Blueray player. The screen came to life and the movie began.

Polito withdrew her laptop from her luggage and turned it on. She cycled through the various programs until she opened her onion browser and descended into the dark web. Moments later a chat window opened up. Polito logged in under the alias *DrCorman*. Seconds later her contact sent the first message.

Saiph:
Your plan to steal the Nestor went poorly.

DrCorman:
There were some complications with your operative.
She made things personal.

Saiph:
We have invested a great deal into this project. We

cannot simply abandon it. We are appreciative of the
intel you leaked to us about Nestor and Morell Blood
but we need more.

DrCorman:
Worry not. I have a backup plan. I always have a
backup plan.

THE END

Mac will return
in
STAND WHERE I'M AFRAID

FROM THE AUTHOR

Five years ago when I first started writing Ben, laying the ground work for what became Never Been to Mars, I'd had the idea for Mac. She was a strong woman, without powers, fighting against the hordes of evil super villains. Could training and skill overcome those with powers? Could someone still succeed when the odds were set against her? These were the themes I wanted to explore but were unable to with Ben. I wanted to explore them with Mac but for various reasons, I was unable to. So Mac waited patiently, sitting on a bench in the back of my head, until it was her turn to shine.

Ben once existed in a different world. He existed under a different imprint and under somebody else's control. Now Ben, back where belongs, returns under my control. This change gave me the chance to expand on Ben, his clan and the dark secrets that exist in his world. This allowed me to finally go to Mac. She was finally able to get off the bench and step into the spotlight.

The Raven was here and both she and I were excited for her arrival.

Now that Mac is out amongst the world, I have many people to thank, for if it wasn't for each of them Mac wouldn't have come to fruition. Each of you played an important part of the Raven's arrival.

To my friends: you are unrelenting in your faith and support of me and my writing. Cliff, Lenny, DeYoung, Chelsea, Kayla and Megan. The only reason I climb so high is because each of you gave me a bump up.

To the Gentle Girls. You have all been there for me and helped in ways I never thought possible. Thanks MM, CL, KF, KC, SC and of course the other MM.

To my family: You are my biggest supporters and critics and somehow that works!

To my Mom: I wouldn't be here without you. Seriously. Not at All. I love you and thanks.

To the real Mac: While Mac and her namesake are vastly different, they are also so much alike. The only reason this Mac was so strong is because the real Mac was so. Thank you for lending me your name and a hint of your power.

Val: You are my one and my only. You are my best friend and my willing partner. I love you more than I love a nice double-decker peanut butter sandwich with a cold can of coke – and you know that's saying a lot.

Zid: I obey your command and do as you bid.

All Hail

Larry Gent
April 2018

My name is Benedict Thompson and I am a superhero. With a single Touch, I can read an item's past. I can tell who used that pen before you, I can describe how that shoe was made and I can describe everything that has been done on that motel room bed.

The problem with having superpowers is that people want you to actually use them.

I just want to watch TV but here I am dealing with a movie-quoting assassin, murderous celebrities, kidnapped children and secret government conspiracies.

My family's in danger, my life is in ruins and worst of all, my TV is being ignored.

I miss my TV.

NOT EVERY
SUPERPOWER
IS A BLESSING

THE BENEDICT FORECASTS

Author **Larry Gent** transports you into a world spies, espionage and superpowers. Each book is an action-packed thriller that'll keep you on the edge of your seat.

Winner of the silver medal in the *Best in Halifax* award, the Benedict Forecasts deleve deeper into the ever growing Lycotta mystery

WHAT'S WORSE THEN BEING STUCK IN A VIDEO GAME AND NOT BEING ABLE TO LOG OUT?

My name is Rake and I'm stuck in a MMO. It wouldn't be so bad if I was in my max level main but I'm not. I'm stuck as my level 1 Rogue. I'm stuck in my bank alt.

Now I'm running for my life, I'm fighting to stay alive and I'm trying to figure out how the hell to get out of here.

Where's a GM when you need one?

HELP!

BEING STUCK IN YOUR BANK ALT!

Vörissa's Catalyst
—ONLINE—

Patch 1.01: New Game+
Patch 1.02: Escort Mission
Patch 1.03: Corpse Run
Patch 1.04: In Another Castle
Patch 1.05: Silent Protagonist

In this new series by Award Winning author Larry Gent, we dive in the action and mystery of the *Stuck Online* genre.

Follow Rake and company as they fight in a harsh digital world. If they're smart, they'll keep their lives. If they're lucky, they'll keep their sanity and if they're both, they just may find a way to log out.

TO ARMS, SOLDIER

LIGHTYEARS TO GO
BEFORE I SLEEP
ON SALE NOW

Allana Guiver was the Legendary Soldier that all of history knew. She won the great war but lost everything she knew and loved doing so.

400 years later, Major Guiver wakes up from cryo-sleep to find a world she doesn't reconize.

Earth is gone, humanity floats through space on a massive ship, searching for a new home and a new alien threat wants to rid the universe of every human.

Humanity needs their Legendary Soldier but how do you ask a woman who gave up everything to give up more?

YOU'RE NOT DONE YET

Photo by Lisa Liteplo

ABOUT THE AUTHOR

Larry Gent is a is a bottomless well of know-legde on historical wars in worlds that are, sadly, fictional.

Larry is a enthusatic gamer whose dreams as a child was to be either a detective or a TARDIS Repair Man (it's like a VCR repair man except you just see the ending of the movie first). He got into writing to give back to the worlds he's enjoyed so much from.

A Perth, Ontario native, he lives in both Ottawa and Halifax where he works as a freelance writer and full-time dreamer. He lives with his wife Valérie and his owner Zid the cat.

Website:	Larrygent.com
Twitter:	@42webs
Instagram:	@xan_in_the_hat

www.ingramcontent.com/pod-product-compliance
Lightning Source LLC
Chambersburg PA
CBHW061305210726
48293CB00003B/1122